THE CUPID TOUCH

GYTHA LODGE

NEVER AFTER

I should have known better.

Not just known better: done better, acted better. *Been* better. There was only ever one way it was going to end.

I've had friends in the past who have told me I shouldn't be so defensive; that I should let people in more. That I'll never be happy until I do. And not just friends. Guys have told me that, repeatedly. The more irritable ones have told me not to be such a bitch, and at the very worst end of the scale, I've been called frigid.

Ha. Frigid. As if there's nothing but ice inside here instead of blazing anger, and loneliness, and years and years of hurt.

Well, I'll take frigid if it means they'll leave me alone. If Luca Veste had called me frigid, I wouldn't have lost a piece of myself. I wouldn't be lying here feeling like my insides had been dragged out through my chest.

The unfairest thing is that I can't even hate him for it.

It's so late into the night that it's almost morning. I wasn't sure there would be a sunrise this morning, but it's already getting dark-blue out there, and I guess the sun will have to come up after that. It always does.

I want to sleep. I really badly want to sleep and not have to wake up, not have to face the world. But I'm so busy missing him that I feel like I'm starving to death.

How's that for pathetic? It's more pathetic when you understand how much I told myself I'd never be this person.

But then, maybe the problem is being any person. Because there aren't a lot of people who manage to get through their life without falling in love; no matter how much they may want to.

And I wanted to. So, so much.

1

DANGER DAY

I hated my alarm that morning. I hadn't slept well, and I'd love to claim it was because I could sense something about to happen. But actually, I'd been up late doing a paper I should have done earlier in the evening. In fact, it should have been done at any time in the previous twenty-four hours. But I'd been busy trying not to think about interviews and my closest friend being on the verge of abandoning me.

The alarm was tuned into Bluesinski, which is generally a good thing. They have a good attitude about starting the morning with upbeat but not-to-loud jazz-funk, and working up to full on hip-hop through the day. Anything wistful or romantic is kept to a bare minimum. That works for me.

But the first thing I heard this morning was host Marty saying "...it may be cold out there, but it's going to be a really fantastic day with the guests we've got lined up in the studio."

"You want to swap days?" I asked him, rolling onto my back and trying to blink my eyes into focus. Somewhere under the sound of the radio, I could hear my housemate, Maria, laughing. Probably because Luke had said something funny. Or maybe just because she was in a good mood. She's been in a permanent good mood ever since the two of them hooked up. Which was back in October. Officially too long for any good mood to last.

Over the radio, Marty was reeling off a lot of semi-famous names with way too much enthusiasm. I wasn't in the mood for chatter.

"Where's the music, Marty?" I asked, before bashing the off-button with a badly-aimed hand.

I was already worrying about Fiona again by the time I was vertical. I knew I was about to lose her. All the signs were there. And it shouldn't have bothered me that much. We weren't even much alike.

You know those people who you meet sometimes, and mostly just listen to? Specifically, to their descriptions of almost-romantic interactions with people. You know? The kind who never ask a question about you, and probably don't know when your birthday is but might just manage a card if Facebook reminds them? The kind of people who are more interested in how hot the logic lecturer is than in any actual logic? Fiona was one of *those*.

But she was smart, underneath all of that. I admired the way she could turn in papers she'd spent half an hour on and still make decent grades. And she was good company. A friendly ear, when she listened. And I actually found myself rooting for her. Wanting her overblown imaginings of romantic entanglements (with guys who probably weren't quite sure what her name was) to be real. I found myself wanting her to be happy.

And that is always, always a mistake.

Today, I felt the sting of that.

The room was still swinging with too little sleep as I started stumbling to the door. I made it all the way to the bathroom door before realising the shower was running.

"Maria?"

I could hear her laughing again, and then Luke saying something. They were clearly in the shower together.

And the only appropriate reaction to that is "Blargh."

I walked away, and then walked back and hammered on the door.

"You guys have fifteen minutes! I'm not being late!"

"What? I can't hear you!"

Maria was as usual trying to hear me over the shower instead of just turning it off for two seconds.

"Fif-teen min-utes!" I yelled, and then stomped down the stairs.

THEY MADE ME LATE. That's the trouble with blissfully happy couples. They don't seem able to remember the ordinary, everyday needs of the other, more irritable people on the planet.

Maria made a vaguely apologetic comment that I usually showered on campus. Which totally ignored the fact that I needed to do other important things: like brush my teeth and pick up my wash-bag, and then pack it all, before I could get on my run-around bike and pound it across town.

I average eighteen minutes to get to campus. It's one of my favourite parts of the day, leaving our run-down apartment on Martha Road and heading south until I can strike out across the river. Even when it's cold, like today, and I'm tired and grouchy, the expanse of the Charles stretching out around me as I cross the bridge is enough to make me smile.

I didn't hang around to enjoy it too much today. I made it in sixteen and a half minutes, including a dangerous race through a just-turning-red light. But by the time I'd chained my bike up outside the Wang center, run to the showers and had the world's quickest rinse, I was still cutting it fine for my first lecture. And of course, I couldn't find my daytime underwear when I dragged my clothes out of my backpack.

"Whyyyyy," I asked whatever fates were listening, and pulled my big stretchy sports panties back on. There wasn't time to check whether the panties showed in the mirror in the corner. I thought they probably didn't, underneath the fairly stiff black pants I was wearing today, but I wasn't sure. Unfortunately, I'd only brought a short jacket and shirt with me, which meant I was going to spend the whole day worrying about having big visible lines on my backside.

I'm pretty sure nobody would credit me with caring about that kind of thing, and it's more than stupid. But sometimes I can be just as vain as everyone else. So I tried not to think about it as I ran flat-out back outside with my helmet banging into my leg because I'd looped it stupidly over my arm.

Generally speaking, I like running a little behind. Being late gives you an excuse to rush past people and be terse without them taking too much offence. (Just to clarify, I don't actually *like* causing offence. It's the unintentional side-effect of being me. Like a more directed form of nuclear fall-out.)

This morning, the I'm-late vibe somehow didn't deter Brad from my coding class coming to jog alongside me. "Hey, Cally. Did you get that VB paper done?"

"Yes." It sounded like a conversation finisher to me, particularly as I made zero eye-contact. But apparently he was either feeling thick-skinned or was desperate today.

"I had a really bad evening," he said, as I turned down Ames Street toward the math department.

"What a shame."

He kept talking, even though I was half-running. "So I didn't get the assignment done. I wondered - could I borrow yours, like... over lunch?"

"No, you cannot."

The Cupid Touch

"Ah, come on! She'll kick off at me if I haven't done it."

I gave him a level gaze. "And that's my problem because...?"

"Help me out here. Please. You're a good person. You let Fiona copy your entire Math paper last weekend." He tugged on his ear in a way that I'm sure would have melted the hearts of most females. Well, most females who like slightly geeky guys in thick glasses. I remained unimpressed.

"Fiona was at her Grandpa's eightieth birthday last weekend," I told him, and turned away. "Not cuddled up in front of Buffy re-runs with Marcie."

There are some things I probably shouldn't say. That was definitely one of those.

"Ah, look." Brad jogged past me and turned around to face me so I had to stop. "I know it's... It's difficult when... I thought we were ok. You know I still care a lot about you."

"And I care a lot about you, too," I said, giving him a big smile.

"You do?"

"No. Now get out of the way."

I barged past him, and into the Ford building. I hoped Brad wouldn't follow me, and I figured I had his terrible work ethic on my side. There were probably two or three lecturers he owed papers to in that building alone.

"Aww, come on, Cally!" I heard him call after me, coming as far as the door.

"Byeeeee!" I called back, and kept walking.

Brad - the ex I should never have tried to get close to - fell away pretty quickly. They do that.

I RAN MOST of the rest of the way to my Math lecture, past the struggle of other students who were running behind. I didn't want to be late today. I wanted to see Fiona for a few minutes before the lecture started, and revel in the last bit of time we'd get to spend together as actual, real best friends. No matter what promises she might make, I knew it was basically over.

But I only made it at the same time Professor Rudnicki did, and had to make do with a wave and a whispered, "My housemate sucks," as I slid into the bench next to her. I could feel the heat coming off me from the combined cycle, shower and run.

Fiona's sympathetic smile was genuine, but I could see she was bursting to tell me something. It made my heart sink a little bit (yeah, I know. It seems unlikely, but I do have one. Two chambers and everything.) I didn't get to hear what it was she wanted to say. The lecture was starting and Rudnicki liked us all to be focused on the board. Listening and taking notes was just about permitted. Private conversations didn't stand a chance.

It was a pretty interesting lecture, as applied math lectures go. But I kept thinking about sitting here on my own next week, or - worse still - next to Fiona while she said nothing to me. Knowing that this was about to happen was never something I could explain to anyone else, either, which made it a lonelier experience.

She was at least still talking to me after the lecture. She grabbed my arm and dragged me outside, then around the corner of the building. We ended up out of sight, but right in a tunnel of wind tearing between two walls. I'd cooled off after the rush to get here, and the after-effects of sweating were making me cold enough already without the hurricane.

Fiona rounded on me, took a look over her shoulder to make sure there was nobody listening (like anyone else was stupid enough to hang around out here - everyone was going as quickly as they could to wherever they needed to be) and then she took a deep breath.

"OK. So there's news." She was slightly breathless in the way she always was when Things Of Significance happened. It was one of the strangely appealing qualities of Fiona that no matter how many times the T.O.Ses turned out to be imaginary or totally unconnected with her, she still went on getting excited about the next one.

"News?" I asked, as if I didn't already know.

"Bethan asked me to watch Alex at football practice with her, and there's a new line-backer on a scholarship. He's transferred over from Princeton and he's hot. Like, seriously hot."

"I heard," I said, trying to match her excitement while I huddled in the arctic air.

"And get this," she went on, with a smile she couldn't quite suppress. "He has a big thing for blondes, so Alex told him to watch out for me, and the guy was really interested. Like, *really* interested. Asking lots of questions and everything."

I gave her as warm a smile as I could manage. "That's great, Fi. So how are you going to get to talk to him?"

"He's meant to be in our coding seminar this afternoon. I actually cannot wait."

She was hopping around, oblivious to the cold, and just as oblivious to the heaviness that was in my chest somewhere. So we had until coding class. And then that was that. She'd be lost to me.

"He'll love you," I told her, and put an arm round her. It was partly an excuse to drag her towards the coffee bar, but there was a lot of just wanting to be part of a hug for a while.

"Well I'm going to go and do my hair and make-up at lunch," Fiona argued, sweeping her blonde fringe to one side and looking up at it. "I wish I'd had a haircut at the weekend."

"Ahh, don't be silly. You look hot."

I squeezed her hard before releasing her and going to warm up before my Math tutorial.

. . .

My math tutor that semester was - and remains - one of my favourite people in the world. At forty-something, Eva Lang had to fight for recognition from high school onwards. It fascinated me, that fight she'd had, and how in the end her brilliance had beaten them down and meant she'd had to be given the Fields Medal and the lectureship at MIT. It felt like the biggest of privileges to have her to myself once per week this term.

I knew that the paper I'd handed in before the weekend had been good, and she confirmed it when I walked in by the way she crinkled up her eyes and said, "Some impressive work, here, Cally."

With a wince, I thought about how she'd react next week, once she'd read last night's terrible offering. I sat myself down, pushed that thought aside, and said, "I really enjoyed it. I've kind-of been waiting to get going on

I'd been looking forward to discussing the last paper with her, but today I was finding my attention wandering. She didn't say anything but after the third time of having to repeat a question, she asked, "Everything ok?"

I couldn't look at her. She'd always been a fan of mine, ever since she'd sat on the interview panel when I applied and fired a lot of questions at me that I'd genuinely enjoyed answering. I'd always been committed to studying, too. It had been a self-defence mechanism through the last few years. When something hurts, work harder.

And then, this week, it had suddenly become just too darn hard.

In the end, I asked a question instead of answering. "Did you ever find that other things just... got in the way of your studies, sometimes? However much you wanted them not to?"

She gave me considering look, and then sat back.

"Many things did. But I suppose I was motivated by all the obstacles that stood in my way. Back when I grew up, girls were not believed to be really fit for the sciences, and Black girls even less so. Every step of the way, they struggled to accept that I had any ability." She gave me a smile that was so confident, I wondered that they had ever been able to doubt her. "Where my male classmates were praised for their brilliance, I was told how good it was that I worked so hard and emulated the other students. They tried to steer me into the arts, telling me I had a good singing voice."

"Did you?" I asked her, curious.

She gave a big laugh. "It was probably the third best voice in my high school. Compared to the math medal I won at seventeen which placed me first in the country. Of *course* I was destined to be a singer..."

She shook her head, and I wondered whether everything was really that different now. I could remember my high school too well, and comments that I was just *working harder* than the boys. That attitude had still been there. They'd called me a "model student," and the most common word on my report cards had been "studious." All except for the report from my beloved discrete math teacher who had written "If Cally ever matches her amount of effort to her vast intellect, she will be defining the course of modern mathematics by the time she is in her twenties." I still have that report card in my bottom desk drawer, for days when I feel like I'm not smart enough.

"But you will struggle, too, I believe," Eva said, "because you are a woman, and because you are a beautiful one. Nobody will want to take you seriously."

I squirmed, my face growing hot. "Oh, I'm not - I guess I waste a lot of time grooming."

"Don't feel ashamed of it," she said, firmly. "You have every right to be a woman as well as an academic. Don't give way to what others think. Just keep on fighting your corner, and make them understand that you're here to make a difference."

I nodded, still blushing. It was partly her compliments, and partly a little shame. It wasn't other people getting in my way right now - it was me.

CONTRARY TO WHAT Fiona had been expecting, everything happened over lunch, before she'd had a chance to groom herself any further. We'd gone to the Sports Centre cafe, which for some reason serves better soup and sandwiches than anywhere else on campus whilst costing less.

Fiona was playing with her food instead of eating it, halfway through some angst about whether she should have worn pink today instead, when I was suddenly, magnetically drawn to look behind her.

He was standing watching her, with a look I recognised only too well. And when she stopped talking and turned to look too, you could have lit a fire off the heat that suddenly existed between them.

"Hey, Fiona," he said. Which confused me. I thought he was supposed to be new.

"Dan?" Fiona sounded more breathless than ever, if that was even possible. "You want to sit down? You look... different."

I realised my mistake at that point. This wasn't the new boy who liked blondes. It was Daniel Fitchett, back from his year working with radio receivers in Nevada and totally transformed.

It was staggering. The nerdy, slightly chubby kid was now tanned and lean, his hair a tousled mess. He seemed effortlessly cool and in fact, exactly Fiona's type.

Except that he was actually looking at her, and knew her name.

Dan hovered, his eyes still locked on Fi, and I got up.

"Here," I said. "You have my seat."

"Are you sure?" Dan asked. Fiona didn't even look at me.

"Of course. Looks like you two have a lot to catch up on."

I lifted my tray, grinned at them both (neither of them looked) and disentangled myself from the chair. I was calm and together as I walked away. After all, you don't live my life without getting good at this.

And that was when the real new boy made himself known by knocking me half-unconscious with a football. Ironically, I didn't even see it coming.

2

SHOOTING THE MESSENGER

"Ah, I... I am so sorry."

I heard him say it, but I was too busy trying not to fall over to look at him. Those footballs look soft, but when they hit you in the face, they *hurt*. You probably already know this. I'm just saying that I had an excuse for both a) staggering and grabbing hold of a student's chair-back, and for b) swearing at the new boy eighteen times in around thirty seconds.

"That's probably fair," he said, after he'd eventually managed to scramble over to me. He bent down and tried to peer at my face, but I turned away to hide the watering in my eyes.

"Eesh.," the guy said. "You have a really big red mark on your cheek..."

It's funny how in that kind of situation the pain makes you really angry, but also makes you feel a lot like crying, which would be actually the worst thing to do in front of a whole cafeteria of sports students. Or maybe that kind of dual reaction is a me thing. I always have seemed to be poised somewhere between rage and despair.

Obviously, I always choose the rage option, because I'm not going to *embarrass myself.*

"If you don't stop talking," I said to the footballer, holding my hand over my cheek, "I'm going to put that ball somewhere unmentionable."

And I turned to look at him.

The feeling was almost as physical as that blow to the head. He was hot, like Fiona had said, but more than that, he was just the kind of hot that I always seem to find attractive. That lean, muscular, slightly dangerous-looking kind of guy with a smile that was just a little bit uncertain, and as sexy as his green-eyed gaze was piercing. And there was a tension to him that implied he was holding something back.

I didn't see which one of the guys it was who muttered, "Watch it. She'll probably do it."

It was definitely the footballer who replied, "Maybe I won't risk it." I could tell because he said it straight at me, quietly.

I'm normally good at comebacks. I mean, I'm not a genius at them, but I'd found that years of snapping retorts at people - mainly guys - had made me pretty decent at firing back something withering. I even represented my school at debating for three years, which is a pretty good way of being smart-talking.

But right then, when I was in genuine need of something genius, my mind was a total blank. Worse than that, I could feel my face starting to grow hot as I did nothing but stare back at him for several seconds.

I had to get out of there, and so I muttered the lamest, "Maybe you shouldn't," and spun and walked away.

I heard him asking someone, "Who's she?" when I was halfway to the door.

I also heard them answer, "Oh, don't even bother. She's out of pocket."

Yup, don't bother, I willed him, shoving my tray away and

escaping through the swing-doors. *I'm just that crazy, cold one to avoid. Don't go there, because it would be bad news for at least one of us.*

I DON'T KNOW if you've ever been ditched by your best friend in favour of a love interest, but if you haven't, it's worth knowing that it's not all that different from breaking up with someone, and both of them are strangely like grieving. You spend the first few days instinctively checking your phone for a text from them, and then wonder what it is that you're checking for. And every so often, you think of something you'd love to tell them about before you remember that you can't talk to them any more.

Every time you remember, it's a little bit like tripping up. Your heart-beat picks up, and you feel jolted; almost scared. And then you carry on walking, a little bit sadder about the world.

Those days are lonely, and make you veer between hiding yourself away, and wanting to reach out to people. In my case, I generally end up phoning my Mom. Which means she generally expects me to have some kind of heartache to spill.

I didn't do it straight away. I knew that calling her would end in a lecture on how to avoid this happening again. But having spent the thirty-six hours after Dan and Fiona fell for each other trying not to lay eyes on them, or the new footballer, or anyone else who had once been close to me and now wasn't, I was aching to talk to someone. So I hid from Maria and Luke in my room, and made myself a comfortable mound of pillows to lean back on while I talked.

She picked up after seven rings, sounding a little distracted.

"Hi Cal. How's it going?"

"Oh, it's... fine. Is this a bad time?"

"No, no," she replied, which I was pretty sure actually meant *yes.* "I'm just giving Fernando a haircut."

"Ahhh. Well, if you need to concentrate..." I was already getting ready to end the call. My mom is the *worst* multitasker.

"I'll just put you on speakerphone," she said, before I could.

I hate it when she does that. It's like being yelled at in a tunnel. And as much as I love Fernando, who is my godfather as well as her new husband and one of the kindest, most patient people, I can't say everything to him that I could say to my Mom.

"Mom, don't worry-"

I could hear her clattering with the phone.

"There you go!"

Bingo. She sounded like she was talking from a cave somewhere in the far East. Just what I wanted.

"Fernando's here too," she added loudly, as if that hadn't been obvious.

"Hi, Cally," he called.

"Hey, Fernando. You still have your head?"

I could hear him laughing. "So far, I think. She hasn't let me check in the mirror, though..."

"It looks great!" Mom argued, and then bellowed, "So how are things?"

I started with my great math tutorial and my good grades, but Mom wasn't fooled. In a short pause, she asked, "How's Fiona?"

"Ah, she's great." I wondered if I should just leave it at that. But I knew Mom would quiz me later if I didn't confess, and I'd probably want to talk about it less another time. So I went on to tell her about Dan.

"So obviously, she hasn't been in contact with me since."

"It's only been a day and a half," Mom argued. "She'll remember you."

"I'm sure she will," I said, doubtfully. "But it won't be the same."

"But that's ok! People pair up. It happens as you get older. It doesn't mean they can't have friends too. Friends are important."

"I know, Mom," I said, on a sigh. "It's just that most people I know seem to get a little... obsessed."

"It's just your age, Cal. Maybe the answer is to be less picky about dating, and then you can hang out together without it being awkward."

I'd argued with her over this so many times before, I couldn't summon up the energy to go through it again.

"I'll bear it in mind," I told her.

"If I were you, I'd go out," she added. "Distract yourself with other people."

I was so far from in the mood right now it was almost funny.

"I have to study tonight," I told her. "But there's that big scholars dinner on Friday I guess."

"Ohhh, you'll need a new dress!" she enthused. "Fernando, can you transfer her some money...?"

"Sure," I heard him say, and neither of them heard my feeble attempts at arguing. The truth was, getting dressed up so I slayed and going out *would* make me feel better. And the scholars dinners were usually fun, populated with some pretty smart and pretty weird people. The conversation was never shallow, even if sometimes it focused a pretty intensively on someone's thesis and not all that much on, you know, actual people stuff.

To me, just now, that sounded perfect.

"Are you sure?" I asked, once they'd finished discussing adding a little bit so I could get a haircut.

"It sounds like you could do with a little pampering," Mom said. "OK, done! The money's in your account." And then she laughed in a way that told me Fernando had grabbed her.

"OK, I'd better go," I said, loudly. They just about remembered to say goodbye.

I spent a while before bedtime looking up dresses, earmarking the stores I really wanted to go to. And then I booked a haircut and slept thinking positively about the next few days in some small way. The dinner was a distraction, and it was safe. It wouldn't mean getting close to anyone who was going to break my heart all over again, or having to watch my best friend smooch with her new love interest.

As it turned out, I was only right on one of those counts.

3

HOW TO MAKE MERRY

I went a little crazy over that dinner. I managed to partition my mind off neatly, so that the only things I thought about were work and looking totally perfect. Coldly perfect, in fact. I don't know whether it was a subconscious manifestation of my desire to keep everyone at a distance, but the dress I found was an ice-blue, full-length gown which made me look the part of the ice queen.

And then I added to it, making myself icier with a cascading crystal necklace with wires so thin you couldn't see them - it looked like my skin was sparkling - and crystals twisted into my hair, which I piled up and secured rigidly. I matched the colour of the dress with a palette of breathtakingly expensive Dior colours that ranged from dark blue right up to shining, glittering white and spent most of an hour applying them in a smooth blend from dark inside my eye to pale white above and outside it. The only dark features were my eyeliner and my mascara.

The overall effect was about as warm and approachable as most people thought I was. In fact, if I had blonde hair instead of brown, and then ventured outside in a snowstorm, I might have actually vanished. The thought was both funny and slightly scary; scary because for a milisecond, it actually sounded tempting.

"You need to get a grip," my reflection told me. I believed it. It looked like it meant business. I settled for picking up my purse in a grip like a vice and holding it like that the whole way into the waiting cab.

THE WHOLE PLACE SHONE. I've always been regretful that MIT is largely modern, with very obviously architecturally designed buildings with weird angles thrown around the place. When I was in high school, I dreamed about a neo-gothic campus with huge trees; and then when it came to it, I chose the place that was going to give me the best chance of getting hired by NASA. Which was still pretty small, all told, but I've always believed it's better to aim high and fail spectacularly.

The newly-completed Manners Building had something about it, though. Maybe knowing that it had come in at twice the budget it was supposed to added to its charm. Definitely, the fact that it was made almost entirely of glass had an impact. And maybe the dark blue sky and emerging stars gave it a little magic. But for just a minute, as I walked into the foyer where the fifty or so guests were being served champagne in glittering glasses, I could imagine that I was an ice queen who'd finally found a palace.

And then I winced at the thought that I might start singing something from Disney, and told myself to get a grip.

There were a few people there that I knew, and a lot that I didn't. I recognised Marcie from my coding class, and a clutch of people from the film society. They were the kind of people I usually gravitated towards: the kind who were friendly enough, but not natural socialisers; the kind who always kept you at arm's-length.

But even as I smiled at a few of them, I didn't approach. Not just yet. I wanted to keep that fairytale feeling for a while longer. So armed with a glass of champagne, I wandered to the emptier side of the hall and spent a good five minutes doing nothing but stare up at the incredible light feature overhead.

It looked like somebody had spilled a metric ton of tiny white bulbs and frozen them in what looked like a swirl of ice as they fell. Parts of the ice-glass sculpture were clear, and others were a warm yellow, which lent colour to the lights, too. I didn't even notice anyone coming up to me.

"Do you think yellow ice is like yellow snow?" a thoughtful voice said from over my shoulder. "Because someone should probably tell them before it thaws."

I didn't need to recognise the voice. I knew who I was going to find when I turned around. It made my heart sink and race all at the same time.

"Wow," I said, to the football star. "Nobody ever mentioned you were a patron of the arts as well as a jock. I would have made more of an effort earlier."

He gave me a slow smile. "I have hidden depths. Which goes for you, too. That make-up job is flawless. You'd never know you have a bruise the shape of a football under there."

I narrowed my eyes at him. He was making it pretty easy to be angry with him. But somehow it wasn't the helpful kind of angry.

"And you're here why?" I asked.

"Well, you know. Scholars dinner, here on a scholarship..."

Damnit, was my main thought. I should have thought of that. But sometimes I forget that not all scholarship students are the academic kind.

"No," I countered, determined not to show that I was disconcerted. "I mean why are you *here*. Within a ten-metre radius of me, when there's a whole room to stand in."

"Ah, I see," he said. He didn't seem even slightly bothered by how prickly I was being, or by the way I was giving him a dead-eyed stare that obviously wished him gone. "I'm new here, so when I saw you hanging around, I thought, 'Hey, great. A friendly face.'"

I had to turn away. It's impossible to keep sending fuck-off signals when you're trying not to laugh.

"That's weird," I muttered. "I think I forgot to bring mine."

"It's ok, I can show you how it's done," he offered. "There's this thing people do called smiling..."

He tailed off because, at that point, Marcie came over with a wiry, tanned guy I didn't recognise. She looked pretty in a pale pink dress that fitted her curvy frame well, and had curled her hair elaborately. Only the glasses she was still wearing made her recognisable as the star of her Twitch channel dedicated to speed-running any video-game going.

"Hey, Cally! Sorry for interrupting, but - oh my God, you look amazing." And she really seemed to mean it, too.

"So do you, Pretty Pink thing." Unbelievably relieved to see her, I leaned in to give her a hug, which clearly took her aback. We weren't really at the hugging stage of friendship. I couldn't help looking at the new boy as I released her.

It was obviously a challenging, slightly smug kind-of-a look.

"So you *do* know how it's done," he said.

Marcie gave an awkward laugh, and then immediately introduced her friend with an abrupt wave. "This is Maurizio. He's on the computer science program at Harvard."

I gave him a smile. "Cally. Nice to meet you. Are you a gaming friend?"

"Right on," he said, and gave a slightly snorting laugh. It

made me smile more warmly. Another geek who could talk about his favourite subject and fail to notice everything else.

There was a brief silence, and then the new boy leaned forwards as if I'd introduced him and said, "Loco."

Who the hell is called Loco? was my principle thought.

I raised an eyebrow at him, but he looked blandly back. And then I realised I was giving him too much attention and looked away, at the gradually swelling crowd. A trickle of people were making their way upstairs to the gallery, where the dinner itself was. Which meant I was nearly free to get away from this persistent, frustratingly handsome, probably-not-even-that-smart football star.

I heard Marcie introducing herself, and then adding, "So are you visiting for the weekend?"

She thought he was my boyfriend. Why does everyone think I have to have a boyfriend? I wanted to wave my hand in her face and tell her I existed in my own right.

"No, no, I'm a student here, I promise," he said, with a laugh. "I just transferred from Princeton."

"Wow, they must really have wanted you. What's your major?" Marcie asked, curiously.

"Ball skills," I muttered, just before Loco said, "Biotech. As far as I know. Haven't made it to all that many classes yet."

I sighed. "Who's the cool kid?"

"Do you want another glass of wine?" Marcie asked, quickly, probably trying to defuse the situation before it became an actual argument.

"Ah, don't worry. I think we're heading up to eat," I told her.

I threw the rest of the champagne back, and started to move off towards the stairs. I was trying incredibly hard not to look at the new boy, but I was intensely aware that he had taken a few quick steps after me.

"I'll follow you on up," he said, as he drew level. "I'm sitting next to you."

I know people assume I don't care what anyone thinks. It's all because of the sarcastic comments, the looking daggers, and the sighing. But I do care, really. And I cared a lot about what he was thinking when I answered, "You have got to be fucking kidding me."

4

NOTHING BUT CHARM

I shouldn't have drunk anything. It's incredibly obvious in retrospect. To be honest, it was probably pretty obvious at the time. It was like getting drunk before an exam. It may have made me feel better, but it was only going to make things a whole lot worse.

The trouble was, I was trying to drown out my hyper-awareness of Loco sitting right next to me. I was trying to numb the little squeeze my stomach gave whenever he said anything, and my electric sensitivity to the occasional moments when his sleeve or his leg brushed against me.

All of it spelled out danger. Danger, danger, danger. I knew where this kind of feeling lead, and I didn't want it again.

So I sank glass after glass of white wine, and spoke ever more energetically to the bio and math scholars sitting to my left and opposite me. But the wine didn't work, and somehow everything I said to everyone else was really directed at him. I was simultaneously trying to challenge him, trying to make him dislike me, and really wanting him to like me a lot. It was not a rational mindset, but in my defence, I know a lot of people who don't know what they want when it comes to possible romance.

Along with all of that, I was listening to what he was saying, alert to any complaints about me to his neighbours. But he was chatting to them nicely, making them laugh and generally acting like a halfway decent human being.

I was so busy thinking about Loco, in fact, that I failed to notice how I was coming across to the bio student with the side parting who was next to me. I was turned towards him, talking animatedly, shifting a little closer every time I managed to touch Loco's leg or arm, and making a point of laughing at his jokes.

See? I was saying in my head to the football star I was ignoring. *I'm not a bitch. I just mean it when I show disinterest.*

I was engaged in a mild argument about appropriate funding amounts with the bio student - whose name was possibly Marty, possibly nothing even close - when he suddenly leaned across and brushed my hair out of my eyes. I fully expected him to at least sit back afterwards, but instead, he slid his arm down to rest on my shoulders.

You're an idiot, I thought. Not at him. Of course he thought I liked him. How was he supposed to know the complex internal dialogue that was going on about the guy I wasn't even talking to on my other side?

I did what I always do in those situations. I gave a cold sort of smile, and moved away until he had to take his arm off. The only way to turn now was dead-center, and it was like Loco had been waiting for this.

He leaned fractionally towards me and said, very quietly, "Hard to tell the impression other people are getting sometimes, isn't it?"

It wasn't even a gloat, or a tease. It sounded like sympathy.

"I don't know," I said, feeling immediately argumentative for some reason. "I usually have a pretty good idea. It's easier when you're universally horrible."

"Not universally," he argued back. "Your female friends clearly like you and you can talk quite nicely when you want."

"That's the thing," I said. "I don't normally want to."

"So it's just about stopping anyone getting close," he went on, as if I hadn't spoken.

"No it isn't."

"Looks a lot that way from here," he said, and held out a plate of truffles towards me. Were we on coffee and chocolates already? I looked down at my empty place in confusion. There was just a single coffee cup now, half-full. I had no memory of two courses.

"Who cares what it looks like to you?" I asked, and folded my arms, ignoring the chocolates despite really wanting one.

"You do," he said, and I made the mistake of making eye-contact with him. He was looking at me steadily, his pupils large and dilated in his very green eyes.

I could feel that gaze all over. I might as well have forgotten all the make-up and the armour; even the pale blue dress and the shoes. I felt like he could see me, totally undefended. And in return I could see him.

I don't know which was more of a surprise: feeling like I'd been caught out and understood, or seeing clearly that there was a shadow over him. Underneath all of the banter and the apparent self-confidence, he was somehow fragile and sad.

Music started up somewhere. Downstairs, I guessed, where there had been a drum-kit and music stands set up.

"Come and dance," Loco said suddenly.

It shouldn't have made me panic, but he was still looking at me with those steady eyes. "We have to wait for the speeches," I said, when I should have just said *no*.

"They had them before dessert," he said, with a sideways grin. "Come on. Nothing to stop you."

He put the truffles down, and picked up his wine-glass to

The Cupid Touch

drain the last of the red he'd been drinking. I wondered if he'd had as much as I had, but I suspected he hadn't.

"I don't want to," I said, quietly.

All he said was, "Yes you do."

And he stood, and held his hand down towards me.

I think if he'd been more insistent - had grabbed my arm and tried to drag me, or argued with me more - I would have resisted. I'm used to resisting, and I know how to make it awkward for someone to try to force you into something.

But he gave me a choice, and with the warm haze of the wine through me, and that look still burning between us, I made the wrong decision.

I took his hand, and let him draw me easily to my feet.

5
THE TROUBLE WITH LOSING YOUR BALANCE

Loco turned out to be a terrible dancer. I mean, actually awful. He had some kind of rhythm, but he had no idea what to do with his arms and legs, or whether to lead or follow. And it didn't seem to bother him at all.

You would have thought that awful dancing would have put the nail in the lid of any chance of romance. It should have done. Except that I started to find it funny.

"What's wrong with you?" I asked, after he crashed into someone behind him and dragged me around so I also crashed into the other half of the couple. I was trying to scowl at him, but for some reason, my mouth kept wanting to smile.

"Aren't you enjoying it?" he asked, with a grin, and twirled me around so hard that I lost my balance and had to grab onto him.

"Of course I'm not," I said. Whilst laughing. Damnit. "You dance like my grandad."

"What are you saying? I'm as swift as a fox." He paused for a moment. "An old one. With osteoporosis. Run over by a 4x4. Ten days ago."

I gave a proper all-out cackle, then got it under control

again, but after a couple of minutes of Loco flinging us into people and apologising and pulling not-really-sorry faces at me, I wasn't even trying not to laugh any more. I was his ally in terrible-ness, and the startled, sometimes amused and sometimes really *not-amused-at-all* faces became something to enjoy.

I told you I was drunk.

I got to the point after about fifteen minutes of this where I was laughing so hard I couldn't breathe properly, and my eyes had started to tear up. That was bad news for my carefully applied make-up.

"Come on, stop it," I said, eventually, pulling a hand free and trying to wipe the tears away. "I'm about to cry all the prettiness away."

"Oh, you mean I'll get to see the terrible, wizened face underneath?" He squinted at me. "I think I can take it."

He tried to pull me onwards, but I resisted.

"OK, I can be less hilarious," he said, and took my hand more gently. He stepped towards me, until we were standing close, but facing each other, our bodies all but touching. And I wished I'd kept my mouth shut.

"Better?" he asked, quietly, twining the fingers of one hand gently through mine. His other arm slid around my waist, finding no resistance on the sheer silk of my dress. We were touching, now, from our thighs, right the way up to our chests. And I could feel it from my breasts to somewhere deep inside.

"Um... I don't..."

My legs and arms chose to let me down completely at this moment. While my brain was shouting at them to move, they seemed to be quite happy where they were, swaying slightly with him in time with the music.

Come on, come on, my brain said. *Shrug him off and walk away.*

"So what is it?" he asked me, quietly, fixing me with that gaze of his that made me feel weirdly anxious. "Are you afraid of getting hurt?"

"Why shouldn't I be?" I asked, a little aggressively. It was a shame I didn't think that one through, though. It told him a lot too much.

"Because not everyone is out to hurt you," he said.

I broke the gaze. I couldn't stand the intensity in it just then.

"Nobody means to," I muttered.

"Some people are a lot more careless than others, you know."

I hate it when people try to argue with me over all this. I'm so tired of it. Everything they say makes perfect logical sense. The problem is that none logic applies to me. None of it. And not because I'm special, or because I think people treat me in a different way, either.

But just then, I was tired of resisting, too. I was hazy with alcohol and aching to touch someone.

That isn't even true. I wasn't aching to touch someone; I was aching to touch *him*. It was Loco who had set up that deep need in me. It was stronger than I could ever remember it, and I should have been stronger in response. Instead of which, I rested my head against his chest, and said, "Aren't they?"

"No," he whispered, into my ear. It sent gorgeous shivers down me, the feeling of him breathing on my skin. "I'm not careless. I can never be careless."

"Why not?"

"I've learned my lesson too well," he said. Then, after a pause, "I've hurt people too much by not thinking. And I'm never going to do it again."

I pulled my head back and looked up at him, momentarily finding the strength I should have found earlier in the evening.

"Yes, you will," I said, and I pulled myself free. It was like tearing myself out of warmth into coldness. "You won't have a choice."

I felt so old as I turned away from him. So old and so tired. But my eyes were already swelling up like a child's, and spilling over.

"Cally, wait," he said. For a second, his hand tightened on mine, and I thought he was going to stop me from going. I almost wanted him to. But then he let me go.

"I'll see you soon," he called after me, as I pushed past all the swaying couples without looking back.

6
THINKING LIKE A TRAITOR

It took me a long time to sleep that night, despite all the alcohol I was saturated with, and which made the room spin whenever I tried to lie down. Undressed, with my make-up only half-removed (and most of that washed off by crying) I tried very hard to sleep, but even with my foot on the floor to stop the spinning, I wasn't able to black out and just forget it all. I kept thinking about him, and about how it had felt to dance with him.

Maria knocked at around eleven whilst I was still lying with the light on. She stuck her head round the door with her black hair all tangly and her pyjamas on, and I wondered whether Luke had only just left. But it was nice to see her alone, without him. It didn't happen all that often, so I asked her in and sat up for a while.

She came and perched on the bed, her legs drawn up, and rested her chin on them. She had a kind of rabbit cuteness that made me want to hug her, too. But I told myself off inside for being a sad, lonely old spinster. Human contact wasn't everything.

"So. How was it?"

She'd spared a few minutes to tell me how great I looked earlier in the evening, which I'd appreciated. But I realised she was now expecting me to have hooked up with someone, or at least flirted with someone. I couldn't admit to that right now.

"It was fine," I said, with a slight shrug. "I talked math and biochemistry with a few people, and then knocked into some people trying to dance."

"No tea to spill?"

She looked up at me, kind-of sneakily. I wondered if she knew, somehow. Had someone called her up to tell her about how I'd danced with Loco? There was nobody there that I knew from her circles, but that didn't mean there wasn't someone there who knew her.

I shook my head at her. She might be giving me a meaningful look, but I was good at keeping all my feelings quiet.

"I drank about four times the amount of wine I should have," I said. "But that's about it."

"OK." She sighed, and seemed to take me at my word. "I hate it when there's no tea."

"I keep meaning to ask how long you're staying up for," I said, changing the subject quite deliberately. "Are you going to be here after the semester?"

"Oh yeah," she said, suddenly enthused. "I'm here for five days, and then my family are taking me ski-ing. I haven't been in two years, and I'm going to be totally lame, but I love it even when I swallow more snow than I ski over."

"That sounds great," I said, and realised it meant I'd have the house to myself for a full week before I went home to spend the festive season with my family. In any other mood, I'd have been looking forward to it. But right now, it sounded lonely.

"How about you?" she asked, nudging me with her toe. "Going anywhere lit?"

"Ahh, that'd be a no. My programming project needs the

computer lab. I'm going to be lucky to get it done by the twenty-fourth."

"Couldn't your step-dad just buy you your own computer lab?" she asked.

"He probably could. But I wouldn't let him."

Maria gave a huge, drowsy yawn, and then stood and shuffled to the door.

"Sleep well, Cinderella," she said.

"Screw you, Pocahontas."

Maria laughed and closed the door behind her.

I missed Maria. I mean, not just when she left the room. That would be weird. But how it was before she and Luke paired up. The time when we were the best of friends, and only left each other to sleep or go to class. I missed how laid-back she was, and how much we could make each other laugh.

I looked over at my phone. I was willing to bet my Mom would be happy to take a call from me. I'd bet, if she remembered it around her own pretty hectic life, that she would want to know how the dinner had gone. But the things she'd want to know were exactly the things I couldn't talk about. Things like whether I'd met anyone nice (debatable) and interesting (unfortunately, that was a yes) and whether I'd danced with anyone (which wasn't exactly dancing, but was definitely touching, and enjoying it, and I wondered if he'd ended up dancing with anyone else and I hoped-so-hoped-not, tried not to think about banging his head together with the head of any girl he decided to dance with…)

"Ahhh, stop it," I said to myself, and buried my head under a pillow. About an hour later, I gave up and rooted out two fresh cryptic crosswords from the pile of newspapers under my desk.

I have a secret passion for crosswords. They're like work, only not. I can lose myself in them, not seeing the words as words, but as signs and clues.

It worked pretty well in the end. After working my way through eight clues, I fell asleep. At least, I assume I did. I woke up at nine with my face pressed on the letters and their reverse images smudged onto my cheek.

IT WAS impossible to sit still that day, and I didn't even have any work to do. I'd spent so much of the past week burying myself in it to convince myself I wasn't lonely that there was nothing left undone except the upcoming project, and I had to wait for my tutor to give final approval of my title. I'd even done the corrections on my awful paper of the previous week, which Professor Lang hadn't actually been all that disappointed in.

So I needed something to do, and given that it was a fine if breezy day with no snow on the ground, that something was going to have to be cycling.

I used up a good hour eating breakfast, locating my kit and making myself lunch to take along in my panniers. After I thought I was ready, I realised I'd better take waterproof trousers and my really thick high vis jacket in case it got wet later.

And then, with a feeling like leaving everything that was difficult behind, I wheeled my bike out of the car-port and joined the moderate traffic leading over the river.

IT TOOK fifteen miles to get my brain to shut up. Every cyclist coming the other way looked like Loco today, which set my heart pounding every time. Sometimes, when they got closer, they turned out to be women, which just went to show what an idiot I was being.

By the time I reached the quieter roads beyond Medford, though, my heart was having to work hard enough on its own to keep that from happening. A moderate hangover makes cycling about fifty percent harder over the long haul, and I started to zone into the rhythm of pedalling. I focused on being efficient; on engaging my abdominal muscles; on keeping a consistent pressure throughout each cycle of the pedals; on using my hamstrings and my quads equally. Little by little, I was leaving all those confused, exciting and painful thoughts behind and being nothing more than a girl on a bike.

I looped up through pretty Lexington and then struck out towards the Howard Parker. It's probably my favourite place close to Campus, a state forest where you can disappear down trails that skirt round lakes and glades. I didn't stop once in the three hours it took me to get there, and by the time I did, I was tired enough to need a really long break.

I took lunch on some of the smooth grey rocks that tumble towards one of the waters, and then lay back on them and rested. Even with my extra layers put on, it was a little chilly until I added the high vis jacket. It was one of those times it would be better to keep going and not cool off, but it was easier just then to lie back and let the end of the hangover drift away.

AFTER BEING SO good for three hours, I figured I had this whole Loco thing nailed. I didn't need to think about him - I just needed to do the things that made me feel good and I could forget about it all.

It was only whilst idly thinking about how it would feel to work in Comms at Nasa that I realised I was imagining all the astronauts with slow, dangerous smiles and messy hair. And then after that, it got confused as I became an astronaut myself, and Loco and I were alone in a space station, miles from anywhere, drifting closer and closer together in the endless cold of space.

. . .

The Cupid Touch

I WOKE up in near-darkness with a shock. I was freezing cold, and realised I had been shivering in my dreams for a while. I staggered to my feet, stiffly, and went to get more of my kit out before realising I was already wearing all of it.

And then I realised something a lot, lot worse. My lovely slimline back wheel was sitting on a totally flat tyre, visible as a useless slug underneath it even in the twilight.

"Shit," I said. "Shit, shit, shit."

I knew as soon as I saw it that I hadn't brought my puncture repair kit. I'd gotten so used to the expensive new tyres Fernando had bought me earlier in the year that I'd started to assume punctures no longer happened.

"What were you thinking?" I asked myself, and threw my bike down in a full-on rage. This was not the time or the place to be without a bike. I'd seen three people in all my time in the park, and I was twenty-five miles from home, without so much as a bank card. Whyyyyy hadn't I added my cards to Apple pay yet? I'd put off doing it for actual years, and now here I was. Stranded.

It was one of those situations that tests your desire to be independent. It's something I've always prided myself on, the ability to get out of things on my own, without needing to ask for help. But then there's being freezing cold, and grittily tired and hungover, in the middle of nowhere without the means to get yourself out of it.

I picked my bike up again, apologised to it for throwing it in the first place, and pulled out my phone to dial my Mom. I started walking as I went, and couldn't help looking around me every few yards to see if there was anyone trying to sneak up on me.

There was no answer: not from her or from Fernando. I tried Maria after that, but it was the same story, and Fiona was evidently too busy with the new love of her life to pick up too. Which left me just about out of options.

In desperation, I tried Brad (whose number I'd failed to delete when we broke up) and then everyone else over again when he didn't reply either. By then I was almost at the edge of the park, and coming up on the long, straight road back to Boston.

I looked down the long length of it towards Boston, and then back up it. There were a few cars coming my way, spaced-out up the rise. I was almost as nervous of who might be in them as I was of being on my own.

I unlocked my phone again, thinking that there had to be a bus. I started walking, anyway, and was alarmed to find that my teeth were actually clacking together as I shivered. It must have turned into a colder night than I'd thought.

The first car swished by me, brightening and then darkening my little world for a moment. I had only a little signal on my cellphone, enough that it took about a minute to load a page with the Boston area bus routes on.

I'd almost got there when I heard the second car. I moved further in off the road, and then looked up at it as I realised that the engine was slowing.

Please don't be some kind of weirdo, I thought. *I just need to get home.*

It pulled up a little way in front of me, the rear red lights slightly dusty. The door opened with a squeak, and a voice called out of it, "Are you ok?"

It wasn't just some kind of weirdo. It was worse: it was Loco.

7
RAINCLOUDS

Ending up in a car with the one person I'd come out here to avoid was not welcome. And yet, of course, it being warm and not the-side-of-the-road-in-the-increasingly-cold-wind was actually very welcome indeed. The fact that it suddenly started tipping it down with rain while I stood there was just another factor.

To clear any doubt up, I did try to avoid it. I gave him a tight smile, and said, "Yes, thank you, Loco. You can run along and be a white knight another day."

He squinted at me.

"Is that Cally?"

Which is when I realised that he hadn't recognised me. He'd just stopped because I was someone out and alone on a highway. And I might have gotten away with it if I'd just said, "Yes, thanks," like any other person.

He turned off the engine and opened the door.

"Seriously," I said. "Did you not hear me say I'm ok?"

He gave a pointed look at the bike tyre, and raised an eyebrow.

"You have a puncture kit?"

I was so angry with him just then. I was angry with him for stopping, angry with him for caring, and angriest of all that he'd seen me vulnerable. It was impossible not to snap at him, even if it just made things worse for me.

"Of course I don't have a puncture kit! Do you think I'd be walking back to Boston if I did?"

"Right," he said, and approached me. I took a step backwards until I realised he was reaching out for the bike.

"What are you doing?"

"Putting it in the back of the car," he said. "You go and sit in the passenger seat and get warm."

"I'm not sitting anywhere," I grumbled, half giving in and half resisting.

It turned out that putting my bike in the back was actually pretty difficult. He had to put two of the seats down, wedge the front wheel in the gap and then twist the handlebars.

"Look, it's clearly too much trouble," I said, four or five times. I was having to hold my teeth clenched to stop the sound of them clacking together, but he didn't say a word. He just kept on pushing the bike gently in until eventually it gave. The trunk shut with a satisfying clunk, and he nodded.

"Come on."

He climbed back into the car, and I finally had to admit that I was beaten. I went to the passenger door and got in, huddling in the seat while he got the engine going and turned the blower on. It was a pretty old, pretty minimal kind of car but at least it had heating.

"I have some dry clothes in my bag," he said, as he pulled out onto the road. "It's only five minutes to a pretty good diner."

"I'm fine," I said, hunching my knees up against my chest. "Just take me home."

He gave a quiet laugh.

"You know, it doesn't make you weak needing someone's help once in a while."

I didn't have a smart reply, so I sat and shivered for five minutes until he stopped at the diner, which looked so brightly-lit and warm that it was like an oasis in the night. But going in meant eating with him. It meant talking further with him, and letting him past more of my defences. It would be a mistake. If he wanted to talk about weakness, that would have been weakness.

"Well, I'm going in," he said, as I sat in mulish silence.

I'd like to pretend that it was only the cold that made me follow him inside. It was definitely a strong motivating factor. But the way he quietly picked up his kitbag from the back seat in case I needed it meant something to me. The truth was, this guy pulled at me as much as the lights and the warmth.

I got out in silence, and took the bag when he handed it to me.

"I can get us a table while you change, if you like," he said, and I was so eager to peel off the wet clothes I was wearing that I didn't even argue. I took the bag and almost ran toward the restrooms, nearly taking another customer out with the bulky bag as I rushed by.

Of course his clothes were too big. I pulled two pairs of jogging bottoms out of the bag and in spite of the shuddering cold, rejected them pretty quickly after it turned out they made me look like a marshmallow. (I told you I was vain.)

Even his skin-tight football trousers (which were clean, thank goodness) were loose, but at least they stayed up and made me look like I had some kind of a physique. I pulled a blissfully dry shirt over the top, which came halfway down my thighs, and finished it off with a hoodie that was roughly two foot wider than I was but was all there was. I thought about stuffing my clothes back inside his bag, but didn't trust myself not to forget them, so I just rolled them all up into a wet, clammy ball and carried them out under my arm.

Loco had secured a table right next to one of the fan heaters that was keeping the place steamy in a humid kind-of a way. He glanced up at me and then looked down at the menu, grinning slightly.

"What?" I asked, dumping the kit-bag down on the floor.

"Nothing at all," he said, and then, with a crooked smile at me, "You're just a lot fluffier-looking than I'm used to."

"Shut up," I said. And then, realising it was a little ungrateful, added, "Thanks for the clothes."

I moved my chair as close as it would go to the heater, hoping that the hours of cooling down whilst sleeping would be undone by a few minutes of intense cooking myself. I was still shivering, but my chest no longer felt like ice. I guessed my core must be warming up a little.

A teenage waiter came over to take our order, and I made an effort to smile at him when I asked for, "A pizza and the biggest, hottest latte you've ever seen."

"Great. Do you want to order a starter?"

I glanced down at the menu, and then back up at him. "What will get the food here the quickest?"

"Ahhh... I guess having a soup starter or something before a main."

"Then I'll have that," I told him.

Loco sat watching me after that. It was kind-of awkward, the way he looked me over, then away, and then looked at me again. But it was better than talking to him and risking getting to actually *like* him.

Eventually, after his coke and my coffee had been deposited in front of us, he said, "I would like to know why you're like you are."

I finished swallowing several mouthfuls of coffee and sighed.

"Well, Loco, it all started in this big liquid mass. We sometimes call it a primordial soup. Somewhere in there, the first sparks of life began, and then-"

"Or you could just be hilarious all evening and I'll laugh until I hurt," he said, smiling slightly.

"My point was," I said, "that everyone is like they are for a large number of reasons."

"True," he said. "But I get the feeling with you that there's one particularly big thing that's making you..."

"A bitch?" I asked.

"No," he said, considering.

"Horrible? Irritating? Kind-of nasty?"

"Defensive and vulnerable," he said.

"Ah, well analysed, Sigmund."

He just ignored the sarcasm, and went on. "We established last night that you're frightened of being hurt."

"Did we?" I asked. "Do you mean when I refused to dance with you for fear of actual bodily injury?"

"I was thinking of when you refused to say anything that wasn't flippant for fear of actual human interaction," he said back, matching my tone exactly.

It was funny, and it was also so true that it was a little bit painful.

"So who hurt you?" he asked.

I spent a while drinking my coffee again, a sip at a time, feeling it warm me through from my stomach outwards. I wasn't really cold any more, but for some reason I couldn't stop shivering. It was a little bit terrifying to realise that I was poised on the edge of telling him something that I couldn't tell anyone. I had to retreat, somehow.

"I don't - it's not something I like to talk about," I said in the end.

"That's ok. I'm not going to pressure you. But maybe consider whether it's it's *good* to talk about. Healthy."

I rubbed a hand over my wet hair, and looked up at him, properly. There was an intense interest in his expression, but also patience. And something like sympathy.

I shook my head, smiling a little humourlessly. "I don't you'd think so if I did."

"Try me," he said.

"You really want to know?" I asked him, my heart speeding up with the pressure of the words that really, really wanted to be said.

"I do. I'm kind-of nosy," he added.

"Fine." I sat back, and looked at him flatly. "Everyone hurt me. Every single person I have ever cared about has waited until I got really close to them and then abandoned me for someone else. Every last friend, and every boyfriend. And everyone will, without it even being their fault."

"Why isn't it their fault?" he asked. Which wasn't the question I'd been expecting.

"It's not - it's pretty impossible to explain," I said, and realised from his expression that he thought I was being some kind of a melodramatic teenager. "And I don't mean because I'm worthless, or not good enough for any of them, or anything like that. I don't have any *issues* and there's nothing you can fix."

He grinned. "All right, I won't try and fix anything. But you can still explain it."

I wasn't so sure. But I was so very tired of keeping quiet. I was tired of the secret I could never let on, because it would be considered madness - or worse, some kind of *damage* - by everyone I cared about.

"I make everyone I care about fall in love," I said, at last. "It's not deliberate, and it's not something I can control. I don't matchmake any of them. It's not - I can feel it happening. I turn them into some kind of a magnet, and bring their perfect match to them. Or maybe they aren't their perfect match, and I just make them love each other anyway. But it doesn't matter which one. Nothing can get in the way of it. That's it. They're in love... for life."

And I hunched back over the heater, waiting for him to laugh at me so we could get it over with and go home.

8

MAGNETISM

Loco was strangely silent for a good ten seconds. And let me tell you that ten seconds of waiting to be mocked is a really long, frustrating time. I had plenty of time to brace myself for his sudden dislike, and even time to count four heart-beats. Which just goes to show how anxious this waiting-game made me.

I watched his eyes strobe around the room, and a small nod. Then he opened his mouth to say something, and of course, our food arrived.

The young waiter really made an effort. I'll give him that. But for all the effect his questions about sauces and cutlery had on either of us, he might as well have been a background TV. Because as Loco raised his eyes to speak, that same instinctive understanding crossed the gap between us. And for some reason, I could see that he believed me.

Once our waiter had "enjoy-your-mealed" away, I ended up talking first.

"You're supposed to laugh," I said, taking my feet off the chair so I could lean toward him. "Come on, Loco. Follow the script."

I wonder if he could hear that my voice was shaking. I could hear it.

"When did it start happening?" he asked, leaning toward me too. I was still cold - still shivering in his borrowed hoodie - but I could feel my face heating up with the proximity.

"Are you serious?"

"Why not?" he asked, with a small smile. "Come on. Tell me."

It's funny how many times I'd practised saying this to people. It's been something I've wanted to share for most of my life. But it was so unexpected actually being asked that I couldn't figure out how to make any sense.

"Since my Dad - he died. I guess that was it."

Loco narrowed his eyes, considering. "You missed him? And you wanted your Mom to find someone else?"

"Yes." It was a whisper. I hadn't even had to explain.

"Could you do it on purpose?" he asked, glancing around the diner with an expression I could only describe as eager.

"As an experiment?" I asked him. "Do you think that's fair on anyone?"

"Who's going to mind finding the love of their life?" he asked me.

I didn't have anything to say to that, and so I looked around too. I saw several couples, one of whom looked like they could barely keep their hands off each other. The rest looked like they were more in-the-habit than desperately in love. But none of them looked lonely.

And then I saw the diner's host: the slightly soft-round-the-edges head waiter. He was over by the door, pretending to check through the menu, whilst casting glances up at the cute twenty-something couple who kept holding hands across the table, and who were leaning close enough to breathe in each other's air.

I recognised his expression. I knew it was exactly how I

looked when I saw some of the happy couples I'd helped to create. It was sadness; and well-wishing; and envy; and guilt that I couldn't just be happy for them. All wrapped up into one.

Without ever talking to him, I felt for this guy.

And that was it. I wasn't trying to control it, and it was like feeling metal move towards a magnet. It was already happening.

"Are you doing it?" Loco murmured.

"Shhh," I said, concentrating on that magnetic feeling and the rushing acceleration that was coming with it. Whoever he found, they were close now. I wondered if it would be a girl or a boy; young or old; pretty or plain. It didn't matter to me, but I'd never stopped being curious all the same.

She rushed in out of the rain, her hair plastered to the sides of her cheeks and her square-framed glasses steamed up. I saw the head waiter raise his head, and his mouth drop open.

"Is there a phone anywhere I could use?" she asked, tugging the glasses off and trying to wipe them on her short, slightly hippy dress. "I got a flat, and my phone's totally dead. I can't get anything to-"

She finally looked at him, and the words all dried up. It was so cliched that it was almost annoying. At least, it was cliched to me. I guess you get to be pretty unimpressed with romance when you see it as often as I do.

"Of course you can. Come and sit down," he said to her, beckoning her over to a chair. I could see how gently he moved around her tiny form, and how much he wanted to touch her. "But if it's a flat, I'm sure I can fix it."

"You can?" She seemed pathetically grateful, and I couldn't help tutting loudly.

I found Loco grinning at me.

"You really don't like the damsel in distress thing, huh?"

"You were getting that vibe, were you?" But there was something so shiny and excited in his expression that I couldn't help smiling while I said it. And then I finally remembered my soup, which wouldn't be unbelievably hot for that long, and I started spooning it down while Loco watched the waiter and the brand-new love-of-his-life. He was grinning, clearly enjoying it all hugely, as they worked out between them that she didn't really need to go anywhere at all tonight when there were rooms at the inn.

Our own waiter cast them a glance as he brought us our main courses. He looked bemused by the whole thing. It was as though he was seeing a side to the head man that he'd never anticipated.

I didn't need to watch the rest of it myself. I'd seen this so very many times. And besides, there was food to concentrate on. I made serious inroads into it.

Loco stopped watching them after a while, and started looking thoughtfully into the distance, instead. He was clearly thinking something over.

"It's kind-of ironic," he said, in the end.

"That's a big word," I muttered.

"I know some bigger ones," he replied. "How about 'misanthropic'?"

"Ooh, four syllables."

"And look, I can string them together into one sentence." He ate three fries at once, and then, whilst chewing, said, "It's ironic how misanthropic a gift based on love and liking has made you."

I've spent a long time cultivating my hard-ass persona, but it stung to hear him say that. It was like he was assuming that I was as cold and hard as the person I pretended to be. Had he really not understood? Did he think I didn't *like* anyone?

"What is it?" he asked, as I put my knife and fork down. I no longer felt like eating.

"Can we go soon?" I asked him, quietly. "I've had enough now."

"I - sure."

He gestured for the bill in that universal sign-language, and then finally set to eating properly. I watched the head waiter and his new girl instead, seeing the differences in their ages, and in their hair and clothes, and knowing that it didn't matter a bit.

Loco was silent until we reached his beat-up old car. It was still raining, and I pulled the hood up, hoping it would hide a little of my face, too. If I had to feel like he'd hurt me, at least he didn't have to see.

But instead of unlocking the car when we got there, he stopped with the key in his hand, and said, "Did I - Did I say something that upset you?"

"Don't be stupid," I said, flatly and immediately.

"So what's up?"

It's the worst question in the world when you're hurting, and you don't want to show it. I couldn't even tell him I was just tired and cold, because for some reason my throat wouldn't work properly.

"Come on, tell me." He took a step towards me, and I reacted by turning further away. "You were almost starting to warm up in there and act like a normal human being."

Somehow being able to say, "Fuck you," was easier than anything else, but it was a choked-up, tearful kind of a comment.

"I don't believe in the hating-everyone thing, you know," he said, really quietly, really close to my ear. "And I wasn't - I wasn't saying it was your fault."

"Not my fault that I'm such a bitch?" I asked, rounding on him.

Stay angry with him, stay angry, the rational, been-hurt-too-many-times part of my mind told me.

"Not your fault that it hurts every time you lose someone," he said, disagreeing. "Not your fault that you actually care, and that leaves you vulnerable over and over again. And not your fault that you try and protect yourself by pushing everyone away."

"Stop psychoanalysing me," I said, smiling slightly now. I didn't want him to stop. I wanted him to go on talking, telling me that I wasn't a terrible person. And when he lifted my hand and knotted his fingers through it, I didn't want him to stop doing that, either.

"OK," he said, and gave me one of those long, slow looks that did weird things to my insides. "Can I try something else instead?"

"Depends what..."

I'm actually not sure who moved first. It might have been him; and I *hope* it was him. But we went from that poised, charged position to a very different one in a heartbeat.

My arms were round him, and I could feel his hands on my back, pressing me into him. Our mouths were together, a kiss that was so hot and sweet and soft that it stopped every last thought of resisting and being strong.

I don't think I've ever felt such desire for someone. I could feel it in him, too; in the way our bodies were pressed together from our thighs right up to our chests, with his hard-on only a part of the intensity of it all.

It's probably a good thing it was raining, or who knows how out-of-control that car park kiss would have gotten. As it was, eventually the hood was soaked through and I had ice-cold water running down my nose. Even in my weakest moments, I've never been romantic enough to put up with that kind of thing.

I drew back from him just enough to talk.

"Can we get in the car now?" I asked.

"Only if you do that again," he said.

"I shouldn't-"

He leaned in again and gave me one long, slow, lingering kiss before drawing away.

"OK," I relented. "It's a deal."

9

TALKING IT OUT

It was the most strangely charged car-ride I can remember. For half an hour, I broke every rule I have, stroking his hair, touching his knee, sliding my hand under his arm. He seemed to find it as hard not to touch me. Whenever he didn't need both of his hands on the wheel or to change his noisy stick-shift gears, his right hand rested it on my leg, or sometimes at the nape of my neck. Either place made me shiver.

All of this touching went with talking. He asked me so many questions that it should have been annoying, but it was difficult not to want to talk and to ask him things back. He wanted to know if I'd hated him when I met him.

"No," I said, trying not to smile. "In spite of the football to the face."

"That was a pretty incredible shot, wasn't it?" Loco said, with a grin. "I'm still sorry. And also not. At least it made some kind of an impression."

"You mean the large bruise? Yeah, I'd say it was an impression."

I squeezed his thigh, hard, unable to keep from appreciating just how toned the muscle was underneath.

"It was weird, meeting you," he said, slowly. "I could see a lot to you that I don't think you wanted me to. I didn't see someone hard; I saw someone who was hurting."

"Yeah, well, I'd just watched my then best friend pair up with someone, so I wasn't in the best mood."

His hand slid to my neck, and up into my hair. I closed my eyes, knowing I shouldn't be enjoying it, but enjoying it anyway. I wanted it to go on all night. Either that, or for it to step up into some really bad behaviour.

"My turn with a question," I said. "Why did you choose to come here? I mean, it's Princeton. And it's not like you're doing a course that has to be done here."

"The course here is pretty good," he answered.

"When you show up?"

Loco grinned at me. "I do enough to get by. Which is kind-of acceptable when you're supposed to be out on the field six days out of seven. And I have - family stuff."

"Family stuff?" I asked him, genuinely surprised. I suddenly had a sickening worry that this was all worse than I'd thought. "You'd better not have a wife and three children waiting for you."

He laughed, properly. "It's ok. I rarely bother with dating, never mind anything serious. I just mean my younger brother."

"Oh." That was better. "Where's he at?"

"He's at high school in Cambridge."

"Wow, close by."

"Yeah, it's... It's why I wanted to be here. He's been having a rough time."

It was strange to feel a surge of affection mixed with a strange kind of jealousy. I loved that he cared about his brother enough to switch colleges for him. But it was also a reminder that Loco was a real guy, with a real life other than me. It reminded me that he was going to end up caring about someone else more than me.

Just enjoy it for now, I told myself, pushing the thought of the future away. *Just until this car ride ends.*

"I'm sorry," I said, meaning sympathy and not an apology. "And your parents...?"

"Just my mom these days," he said, a little tightly. He drew his hand gently away from my hair. "She has her own stuff to deal with."

I couldn't read from him whether he meant things she couldn't help, or things she cared about more, so I didn't ask him any more. And my curiosity had been dulled a little by remembering how short-lived all of this was.

"What about you?" he asked. "Why are you here? Doing... math?"

"Good memory," I told him, trying to smile. "It's one of the best places to go if you want to do math with computing. And if I don't get where I want to go straight out of here, I'm going to apply for an aerospace postgrad."

He gave me a curious look, and then looked back at the road.

"What do you want to do with it?"

"I want to apply to NASA," I said, with a shrug. "You know how every kid wants to be an astronaut? That's still me."

"Oh, so not so unromantic after all," he said, and picked my hand up and kissed it.

"It's not romantic," I protested.

"Well why do you want to do it?"

"I don't know. I want to go into space. I've been obsessed with it ever since I was a child. I dream about it at least once a week, what it must be like to lift off, up there." We were passing streetlights, now, and the light reflecting off the raindrops on the window could almost have been stars just then. On that night, with Loco there and the feeling of unreality, they could pass for almost anything. "And you know, maybe there's another world out there. One with life, and different laws of physics. One where this shit doesn't happen to me."

Loco squeezed my hand, and then, a few seconds later, at a stop light, pulled me towards him and gave me a sweet, slow kiss that was like a promise. I lost myself in it all over again, and only pulled back when someone hooted loudly from behind us.

LOCO DROVE me right back to my apartment, not needing much direction after I told him the address.

"I grew up here," he said, with a smile. "I haven't been stalking you, I promise. There hasn't been time around football practice."

He helped me squeeze my bike back out, and I let him help a little bit more graciously this time. But I was the one who lifted it up the three steps at the front of my building and propped it next to the door while I found my key.

My hands were shaking as hunted for it. It took me a few minutes to realise that I'd put it in my cycling-jacket pocket. Which I'd left at the damn diner.

"Shit," I said. "Total organisational fail."

"Your key?" he asked. "What... Oh. They're not your clothes."

I leaned to buzz on the buzzer before he could say anything else. I hoped Maria was in. And also, I kind-of hoped that she wasn't. I knew that there was absolute danger in going anywhere with him. And I could feel that both of us wanted there to be an excuse.

"You know," he said, pulling me gently towards him, "you won't lose any independent-woman points if you have to stay at mine tonight."

I could feel my heart thumping somewhere in my throat. I

shook my head, but I reached up and kissed him anyway. It was fiercer, that kiss. It was made up of a lot of wanting and needing.

The intercom crackled and I jumped back, feeling like I'd been caught.

Maria's voice asked, " - I help?"

"Hey Maria," I said, leaning in to speak into the intercom. "I've managed to leave my key halfway to Canada. Could you buzz me in?"

"Sure!"

There was a prolonged buzz, and I reached out and tugged at the door immediately, trying not to look at Loco.

"Shame," he said, very quietly, and just as I began tugging my bike inside, he grabbed me, hard. For a second, he gave me the full benefit of those highly-trained, sculpted muscles as he gave me a kiss as fierce as the one I'd given him. And then he let me go.

"I'll see you tomorrow?" he said, while I tried to manoeuvre my bike through the door with legs that felt like they weren't attached quite right.

I stopped and looked at him, agonised.

"I shouldn't-"

"You should, you know," he said. "You haven't heard my secret yet."

With a last, dangerous kind of grin, he turned and jogged down the steps to his clunky old car.

10

WEAKNESS

I knew that Maria couldn't have seen me on the door-step. Mine is the only room of the apartment that looks out onto the street, and even I can't see who's buzzing. But she gave me a raised eyebrow as she let me into our poky hallway, and I felt like Loco's kiss must have left marks on me, his name blazed across my skin.

"Thanks," I said, trying for casual but talking way too much. "I got a puncture twenty-five miles out and then it started raining, so I found a diner to take refuge in until I could persuade someone to give me a ride home. But I can't believe I left my keys there. What a perfect end to a ridiculous day."

I wheeled my bike past her, and into the tiny third bedroom that was too small to rent out.

"So you got a ride from Luca Veste?" Maria called from behind me.

"I - what?"

I turned round to see her giving me a knowing smile. How the hell had she found out? Had someone seen us together?

"How exactly did you end up wearing his football jersey?" Maria asked. "Was there a little detour on the way home?"

Shit. I'd forgotten about the hoodie. His name was literally written on me.

"No, there wasn't!" I answered, outraged. Then I realised I was almost shouting at her, and that I was starting to blush. "It isn't even slightly what it looks like."

And yet, it was basically exactly what it looked like. Like someone who'd fallen for the college stud and sort-of wanted everybody to know.

"I was freezing cold," I went on, in a calmer voice, while Maria settled in a kitchen-chair to watch me. "I changed at the diner, and left all my wet clothes - and my keys in the pocket - next to the table. He was just helping me out."

"Uh-huh," Maria said, significantly, and then gave me a crinkle-eyed grin. "He going to help you out tomorrow?"

"No," I said, immediately, before remembering that he had a secret, too, that I badly wanted to know. "I might - if he wants to drive me back out to the diner to get my stuff, that would be fine."

"Sure," she said. "Nothing but helpful."

She wouldn't stop grinning at me. It was the same expression my Mom had when I first went on a date, and I knew the expression always ended up in a disappointed one when I had to explain that the dreamboat had gone off with someone else. It wasn't fair to be angry with Maria for reminding me that I was being an idiot.

Luckily for me, Luke called Maria's cell-phone at that point, leaving me free to escape to my room and then beat myself up about being weak throughout a long, hot shower.

I knew I shouldn't see him the next day. But oh, I wanted to.

Just see him one more time, I told myself, *and then you can break things off.*

I didn't want to think about the bit where I started to protect myself again. Even with the hot water pouring over me, it made me feel cold.

Loco emailed me at ten. I got it straight away, because I'd been checking every two minutes since I'd dragged myself back out of the shower. All I'd achieved in the intervening time was three unsent versions of a message to him explaining that I couldn't see him again, and a good twenty minutes of looking at the photos of him I could see on Facebook. However hard I tried, I couldn't seem to convince myself that he was just a brainless jock.

It wasn't a particularly long message:

Hey Cally,

I dug your email off the college address-book. I just wanted to let you know that I'd dropped your cycling gear off. It's just inside the main hall, as some civic-minded neighbour kindly let me in. Apparently I didn't look violent enough to bar.

I think your cell-phone might be in there, too. There was definitely something buzzing, and I couldn't think of much else that vibrates that you might have taken cycling.

I've got practice tomorrow until four. Am I ok to swing by or meet you somewhere at five?

Hope you get that puncture sorted out,

. . .

Loco

x

IT MADE ME SMILE. I hate that.
    It also made me feel bad. He'd driven all the way back out to the diner to get my stuff. It must have taken him an hour. All just because I'd been too wrapped up in agonising over him to pick up my stupid clothes. And they'd probably been damp still, and kind-of sweaty, and he'd had to carry them.
    He's doing it on purpose to make you feel bad, I tried to tell myself. But I was coming to the gradual conclusion that he was just that kind of person. Underneath it all and quietly, he cared about people.
    I thought for a while before composing a reply.

HEY LOCO (ARE you really serious about that? I figured it was just what other people called you. It makes you sound like a Manga character),

THANKS FOR GOING to get my clothes. That's pretty nice of you. I almost feel bad about insulting your name, now I think of it. And let's hope for everyone's sake it was just a cell-phone.

MEETING up tomorrow sounds like a really bad idea. I guess I'm in.

. . .

WHAT DID you have in mind?

H

x

PS - If I'm feeling nice, I may even wash your clothes before returning them.

I SAT BACK and thought about four times about messaging him again to say I'd changed my mind. But by the time he'd emailed back twenty minutes later, I hadn't made myself do it.
His reply was even briefer, with just the one line.

HOW ABOUT SOME STAR-GAZING?

x

I WASN'T EVEN sure what he meant, but I said yes, anyway. I didn't seem much good at saying no to Loco.

I USED up most of the next day on life admin. I did all my laundry, tidied and vacuumed the apartment, fixed my puncture and food shopped. I took advantage of the weather clearing after lunch and went for a run for an hour along the Charles, and then showered. I also, totally coincidentally, gave my hair a really good wash, shaved my legs, moisturised and tidied my eyebrows.

I still had an hour left once I was oh-so-casually dressed up to look as hot as possible, so I called my Mom back. It had been her call that had set my phone buzzing the night before. I felt like a criminal trying to hide what I was about to do from her, but she seemed happy enough to chat about a Christmas plans and what she was buying Fernando.

Right at the end of the call, she said, "It's so nice hearing you a bit more upbeat. Sounds like things are better."

"Yeah," I said, with a little squeeze of my heart. "Yeah, I guess so."

I hung up knowing that this time wasn't going to be any different, no matter how much I might wish it was.

Loco buzzed at five past five. I picked up the bag I'd crammed his clothes into, and tried not to hurry down the stairs. For some reason, my legs were unsteady, like they were when I'd run about twice as far as I had.

I opened the door to him and felt such an intense rush of desire it was frightening. He was wearing Levis and an almost-tight long-sleeve, his hands tucked into his pockets and his hair scruffy. Everything about the outfit showed off the sculpting of his body, and it got a lot more intense when I met those green eyes and could see the same expression in them.

All the oh-so-cool greetings I'd planned went out of the window. Within a microsecond, I was pressed up against him, my mouth meeting his in a hot, wet, unbelievably sexy kiss. I let go of the bag, and pressed my fingers into his taut shoulders. I felt one of his hands come up to my hair and it was total bliss.

We only let up when footsteps announced the guy in apartment two arriving home. We stepped out of his way, and I muttered a "Sorry." But we didn't quite let go of each other, even when my middle-aged and slightly grumpy neighbour huffed at having to squeeze past.

I watched him step over the bag of Loco's clothes, and bent to pick it up.

"I washed them," I said to him, "with the most floral-smelling detergent I could find. Your team-mates are going to love you."

He laughed, which I could feel as a rumble in his chest, and took the bag. "Thank you. I think."

"I put a snickers in there, too," I added. "By way of an apology for dragging you away from the diner before dessert."

He glanced in the bag, and then up at me. "That's almost a nice thing to do. See, I knew you had it in you."

"Don't start expecting it," I muttered. And then kissed him again, briefly, before walking down with him to the car. "I want to know this secret. And I want to know where we're going. Are you going to keep me in suspense?"

"Maybe on one of those counts," he answered, unlocking the car but making no move to get in. He squeezed up against me and I ended up leaning back against the car door, feeling quite happily trapped between him and it. "I figured we'd have time to talk on the way about what it is that I do."

"Hmm," I said, sliding a hand up his side. "This had better not just be a boast about your prowess."

He grinned. "I won't promise that won't happen at some point," he said, "but right now, I was going to tell you - my secret. Which is kind of the flip-side of yours."

He was suddenly giving me an intent look, and I realised that he was serious. That he was telling me something true. It really mattered.

"What do you mean?"

"I mean that you make people fall in love when you get to care about them; I destroy people when I get to hate them."

11

SYNCING

Ironically, given my own bizarre secret, I didn't quite believe him. Though realistically, it was a lot to do with him telling me something that was just like me, only not. It was a little bit like talking to my frankly wonderful stepdad, Fernando. He is amazing in every way, and works harder than anyone I know, but he always seems to have had the same illness as you the week before, only worse. Which always stops you from complaining about it.

I found myself giving Loco a Look.

"Are you *copying* me?" I asked.

"Seriously?" He shook his head with a slight smile. "You, of all people, don't believe me?"

"I do!" I protested. "I just - it's a bit strange is all. That you happen to have a thing that's just the same as my thing."

"It isn't the same," he said.

"Well... Can you show me?"

He huffed some air out, and he was close enough that it was warm on my mouth and I breathed some of it in. It was so sexy, I almost forgot what we were talking about.

"I can't really. I mean - let's drive. I can maybe show you... if someone deserves it."

He stepped away, and I couldn't help a feeling of disappointment.

Get used to it, Taylor, the tough part of me said.

I let myself into the passenger side again, trying to puzzle him out. I felt like this was a joke, somehow. Maybe he thought he could convince me that what I did wasn't real. Which wasn't so very unreasonable. I'd tried to convince myself enough times.

Or maybe he was telling the truth. Maybe he actually destroyed people.

I suddenly found myself wanting to know, quite badly, what that meant. And for the first time, looking at that muscular body, the hard jaw, and the slightly dangerous smile he gave me again, I wondered if there was something a little... *wrong.*

And then he reached over and gave me such a tender, gentle kiss that all of the worry melted right away. I relaxed into him with a sigh.

You're an idiot, Taylor, that same voice said.

Yes, the weak half of me answered, revelling in the warmth of his kiss. *And isn't it more fun being an idiot?*

WE WERE over the river and passing North-West through Cambridge before something happened to wake me up again. It was a stupid, simple thing: a motorist behaving like an idiot. He was a middle-aged guy in a big, new-looking cream Dodge. One minute, he was behind us, and the next, he'd shot past on the inside lane to our right and cut in to the point where Loco had to brake sharply.

"Jeez," I hissed, grabbing at the dash.

I waited for Loco to lean on the horn, but instead, he seemed to have grown coldly focused as the driver weaved again and undertook another driver.

And then I felt something. It was a very, very different feeling to the one I had when two people were about to fall in love. It was a colder feeling and a hotter one at once. It felt like the part in a film where you know something terrible is about to happen, and you can't stop it.

"Him," Loco said quietly, slowing down to leave a gap between us and the cars in front.

There was a brief squeal of brakes, a crunch, and Loco cruised into the inside lane to go past what was now a small pile-up with the guy in the Dodge in the middle of it. As we were passing, the car in front suddenly lit up with flashing blue and red lights, and I almost laughed. He'd driven into an unmarked squad car.

But then I thought about the people in the car behind, too.

"Do you think any of them got hurt?" I asked, craning to look behind me as Loco powered his own old, unimpressive car away.

"Low speed impact, I don't think so," Loco said, and then added, quietly, "I hope not."

It hit me, then, that this was what he had done; this was what he could do. He was revenge, pure and simple. The guy had got what he deserved, as far as Loco thought. But only at a cost to others.

And I wondered how often Loco thought someone deserved it.

Just like that, I was no longer enjoying this drive. I wanted it to stop, so I could get out and away from him.

"Loco," I said, hearing the shake in my voice.

He gave a strange, bitter smile. "I know," he said quietly. "You want out, right? Because you think sooner or later, you'll be the one pissing me off. Or someone you know, right?"

"Yes," I whispered.

"You can get out, if you want," he said, slowing the car. "But will you listen to me first? Just for a while?"

If you want an illustration of mixed-up, the way I felt right then was pretty comprehensive. I could hear the hurt in his voice, and I wanted to comfort him. I could hear the warning sounds of the last few days turn into an urgent, blaring siren in my head. I wanted to ask him question after question about this power of his; find out when and how it had begun, and what kind of a person it made him. I wanted to shout at him for drawing me in this far when I'd told him it was a bad idea. And I wanted him to kiss me again, and again, and again.

I gave in all over again.

"All right," I said. "Talk."

12

A TROUBLED BOY

To Loco's credit, he told it quickly and well. The first part was while we were driving on that North-Westerly path through Cambridge; and the rest happened after we'd pulled into a parking lot and he'd switched the engine off. Not that I noticed that for quite a while.

"I don't even know when it started," he said. "People tell you these stories when you're young, about bad people getting what they deserve. And then in every film, it happens too. I had an inbuilt belief that that was just how things worked. So when someone tripped me up and then they fell down some stairs; or when I got shoved in the cafeteria queue by some guy who just afterwards burned himself on something, it all made perfect sense."

It did make sense, even to me. Listening to him, I could remember vividly how it was when my Dad died. The main thing I kept asking myself, over and over, was what he'd done to deserve it. And when I couldn't find anything, I tried to figure out if Mom or I had been the ones at fault. I'd fixated for three weeks on how I'd been cruel to one of my school-mates until my Mom finally explained to me that it was nobody's fault; that people just died sometimes. I think it was the cruellest thing I've ever had to come to terms with.

"I only started to realise that it didn't work like that," Loco went on, "when I talked to some of my friends. I'd say, all confidently, that yeah, it sucked how someone had been unkind to them or stolen off them, but they'd get what they deserved. It made some of them pretty angry with me after a while, because the big kid who was beating the crap out of them twice a week wasn't getting any kind of punishment. Gradually, I started realising that it was only when I got angry with them, and I could feel it happening when it did."

"What a messed-up thing to realise," I muttered.

He gave me a small smile. "I guess it's a little worse than realising you make people live happily ever after," he said. "Though at that point, I still just thought - well, it seemed like they deserved it all. So it was a good thing."

I started to feel uncomfortable again. I had a feeling he was about to tell me something that was a lot less good. But I wanted to know anyway.

"What changed?"

"Mostly, it was my Dad," he said. And the way he said it was just loaded with emotion. It was like that one word had a whole life's-worth of pain and anger and guilt mixed up in it. And it probably wasn't so different from the way I said the word. "He had what started out as a small alcohol problem. But the thing I've learned is that no alcohol problem is ever small. As soon as it's got you, you start to slide. And he slid pretty quickly, until he lost his job. And then he got... vicious."

Despite all my reservations, I found myself putting my hand out, instinctively, to touch his shoulder.

"We all took it about equally. I mean, I wasn't this size then. I was ten and a lot scrawnier. There wasn't a lot of money spare for food back then. I'd get angry, every time, and I thought if I used this thing I have then he'd start to feel sorry. Now I could tell you that a lot of his problems came from self-loathing, but at that point I just thought maybe he would learn what it felt like. So in small ways, I let him have it. He'd whack his head, or get pulled over by the cops for drink driving, or he'd get mugged and beaten up himself. After a year, he'd decided that the whole world was against him. It was paranoid, and he started to think we were all of us plotting to make him look stupid. He'd accuse us of doing these crazy things to ruin his life, and it was hardest for me to deny it, however crazy he sounded. Because I knew I was responsible. I was - I was terrified of him. And I couldn't seem to control the hatred, either."

It made me feel a little bit sick just hearing it. I couldn't imagine being that frightened all the time.

"What happened?" I whispered, taking his hand and knotting my fingers back through it.

"It actually looked like it might get better," he said. "He finally went too far for my Mom, who was so frightened of him that she felt she couldn't leave. She had no money, but she was still working at this restaurant, and there was a guy there who liked her. He offered to let us all move in with him, away from my Dad, and the manager there went and told my Dad. He was so angry that he went for my Mom like he was going to kill her, and then when my brother and I together tried to haul her off him, he dragged us out to the car and drove off with us. He was blind drunk and I thought we were going to die. But there was that anger there too, and I brought vengeance down on him. He smashed the car up on a bollard, which thankfully fell and didn't damage us too much, and got arrested. It was just the biggest relief when the cops listened to me and my brother, and explained everything. We thought he was going to end up in jail, and my Mom told us that was it. She was leaving him."

"But it didn't work out?"

He shook his head. "It turned out he'd got more money hidden away than he said. He posted bail, and while we were packing our things up, he let himself into the house. It wasn't his usual entrance, all angry and loud. He snuck in there, and before we knew it he had my Mom by the hair, with a knife at her neck. I didn't really have any time to think. I knew I had to use what I had, or he'd kill her."

My heart was thumping in my throat somewhere, and I wasn't the one living through it. He seemed so calm talking, it was surprising. But I guess he'd had time to get used to it.

"He tripped on the stairs while he was trying to drag her down them. My brother had hold of my Mom's arm, and was screaming at her to let her go. So she didn't fall. It was just him. He grabbed at the wall with his knife hand to try and stop falling, but he fell anyway. I knew as he went that it was going to kill him, and just then, I didn't care."

There was a really long, long silence. I didn't feel like myself just then. Sarcastic, unemotional Cally wanted to cry for those poor kids and their Mom. And to hold onto him and tell him it wasn't his fault.

"I wouldn't have cared either," I said quietly.

"But I did it to him, Cally," he said, meeting my gaze. I saw that hurt running deep into him and I finally understood it. "I made him that person. He definitely had something in him that made him want to lash out, but if I'd held back, he wouldn't have ended up that way."

"He might have done," I argued. "He might have ended up just the same, only more slowly. No matter what hand life deals you, you have to be a pretty sick person to take it out on your family," I said.

He gave me a slightly bright-eyed smile. "Who knew you could be genuinely kind?"

"Just my Mom, I think," I said, and ruffled his hair. "I think I've kept it from everyone else pretty successfully."

There was another silence, but this one no longer tense. The air felt so clear in that car, I wondered how I'd been able to bear the fog of secrecy I'd been living in for most of my life.

"So you stopped using it," I said, eventually. "You decided you had to control it."

"Yes," he said, "because I killed him, and no matter how angry I am at someone, I know in my heart that nobody deserves that."

I couldn't help kissing him then. I felt like I could see all the way into him, and that he was good all the way down. As well as a little bit messed up and tortured, which is always pretty sexy, in my experience.

I let up after a passing kid rapped on the car window and laughed at us. I finally clocked where we were.

"Is this the observatory?" I asked him.

"Sure is," he said, flattening my hair where his hands had mussed it up. "So how about those stars, then?"

13

THE MOST DISTANT STAR

You know when you think someone's messed something up, but you really don't want to tell them? That was how I felt walking up to the Smithsonian Institute's Observatory. I'm a geek for everything space-related, and I know that the observatory isn't the telescope a lot of people assume it is. Instead, it's the receiving station for the super-telescopes based out in the middle of the Arizona desert. It's also not accessible to the public.

I smiled a little awkwardly at Loco as he buzzed at the locked glass door. I was pretty certain we were about to get turned away. I didn't mind missing out too much: I knew I'd be likely to enjoy whatever we ended up doing. What I did mind was the idea of seeing him embarrassed. It's probably my second-biggest secret that I hate seeing people hurt or upset. It's probably the thing I hate most in the world just after getting my heart trampled all over.

Life sucks, hey?

The guy on the other end of the intercom, when he patched through to us, was clearly eating something. It was pretty hard to hear anything other than crackle, munch, "in?"

"Hi," Loco said. "It's Luca Veste. Is that Brandon?"

"Luca... Oh. Yeah. Come on in."

I glanced at Loco as the door buzzed.

"Pretty well-connected for a jock."

"Pretty and well-connected," he corrected, and pulled me through the door into a small, very underwhelming lobby that looked about as space-age as my aunt Trish's living-room and which smelled like a student house.

One of the chipboard doors opened and a slim, dark-haired teen-or-something emerged, complete with the most disconcertingly beautiful blue eyes I've ever seen. Despite the side-swept fringe that hung over them and his slightly hunched shoulders and air of uncertainty, I was a little bit awestruck. Where Loco was gorgeous, this kid was beautiful.

"Aren't you supposed to be studying?" Loco asked him, which I admit confused me a little bit.

"I got finished early for the day," the kid said. "And anyway, you can't use Brandon without getting me into the bargain." He glanced at me, a quick, curious look, and then back at Loco. "I didn't know you were bringing anyone."

"Yes, you did," Loco retorted. "This is Cally. Cally, my brother, Axel."

"Hi," I said, holding out my hand, still with that sense of awe. It reminded me of meeting the lead singer of a boy band everyone was into when I was thirteen. All I could see was that pretty face and it made me slightly awkward. And when I get awkward, I naturally resort to some kind of joking cruelty towards someone. "Woah, how come you got all the nice-looking genes? Loco, you need to complain to someone about that."

"I'll see if I can get a refund." Loco squeezed me around the shoulders while Axel gave me a small smile.

"Brandon should be finished with his simulation thing in a sec. I'll see, if you're ok to wait."

"No problem," I said, as he vanished through the door again.

"You're not allowed to fall in love with him instead," Loco said quietly, without seeming to be concerned at all. "Just so you know."

"But he's so pretty," I murmured, and then kissed him on the lips with a smile. Despite all the awe, and his brother's breathtaking beauty, when it came to sheer sexual magnetism, Loco might as well have been the only guy within a square kilometre.

Axel reappeared, looking relieved.

"He's all done. Come on in."

As we entered a dim room with an impressive array of screens, I found out where the student kitchen smell was coming from. Scattered around a series of desks were enough take-away food containers and empty drinks cans to have fed most of MIT.

We also found Bernard, who was alone and apparently oblivious to the chaos.

He was a tall, really slim red-head in thick glasses. He was hunched over a desktop, typing furiously on a keyboard. It looked like he was coding in Visual Basic, at a glance, but so much more quickly than I was able to that it was embarrassing.

Axel went over to stand behind him, watching him patiently as he worked, and then, eventually, interrupting with a slight brush on his shoulder.

Oh, I thought. So that's why we're allowed to be here.

Brandon glanced up, saw Axel and gave him a blank look.

"All ok?"

"Yeah," Brandon said, distractedly, and then glanced at Loco. "Oh. Yeah, sure. I was just - it's fine."

He quit whatever he was doing and swung his chair along the desk to the next machine. As he moved the mouse, suddenly the screens above us sprung to life.

My stomach actually squeezed at the sight. We were looking

at a nebula, a circular, blue and yellow fountain of light blown up on all array to the extent that it looked like I could walk right into it and disappear into the dust clouds.

"Is that the Pegasus Nebula?" I asked, taking an instinctive step towards it and then coming up against the desk and regretting having to stop.

"Ah, yeah," Brandon said, looking at me with what I could see was slight irritation (and I know - I get that reaction a lot.)

"Wait, are you a star geek too?" Axel asked, unfolding his arms and looking like I'd suddenly become interesting.

"Well, I don't know about geek," I hedged.

"She's a geek," Loco said.

"You don't even know!" I protested.

"It's not exactly a hidden quality…"

I tried for A Look, but I couldn't help smiling. It probably didn't help that in the blue-green light from the screen, his eyes almost glowed, and the dim room was making me think bedroom kind of thoughts.

I could see that he was thinking them too, and it was just the sexiest thing.

"Hey, Brandon," Axel said, leaning over the desk. "Show her the new supercluster."

I actually looked away voluntarily from those green eyes. I couldn't help it.

"A new one?"

"Pretty much," Brandon said, trying to sound off-hand but not quite doing it. "Like, this week."

Pegasus' gorgeous rearing head-like clouds vanished as he navigated his way through some complex files.

"This isn't live," he said. "The images were taken Monday to Tuesday and Wednesday to Thursday."

Something sprung up on his screen, and then in a moment was replicated on the array above him.

I stared at it, absolutely fixed on the black and gold image. I knew about those clusters. Our own, Virgo, held some eight thousand galaxies, and was within a much larger one named Laniakea, which held hundreds of thousands.

This was more like the huge supercluster. It had delicate, spreading fingers that must have contained thousands upon thousands of galaxies. It was glorious.

"How far away?"

"Sixty billion light years, give or take," he said, and he finally seemed to be losing his irritability at my excitement. "It hasn't been named yet, but it's currently numbered 989/934."

"Beautiful, isn't it?" Axel said, and put his arm lightly on Brandon's shoulder. I glanced at Brandon, who seemed oblivious as he zoomed in on the brightest part of the image, which was like the palm of the hand.

"It is," I agreed, and felt strangely emotional. Here was a place I was guaranteed never to reach in my life-time, brought up onto the screen via a distant telescope waiting patiently in the night-time of an Arizona desert. All, just now, for me.

I felt Loco move up to stand behind me, and I reached down and squeezed his hand. He squeezed back, accepting, I think, that I was thanking him but unable to look away from it all.

We spent an hour there, flipping through view after view, and after a while, even Loco started to get enthusiastic about it. I found Axel's enthusiasm as great as mine, but I couldn't warm to Brandon, who seemed detached and condescending about it all, however brilliant he might have been.

After the hour, he was clearly getting tired of us, and said he wanted to check on the live imaging.

"What are you looking at?" I asked, not quite willing to enter the real world again.

Brandon paused for a moment, and then gave a small smile and brought up a new image.

I squinted at it, in vague recognition. "Is that the Dumbbell Nebula?"

"Close," Brandon said, and gave me a slightly condescending smile. "Only about six thousand light years off. That's Eta Carinae viewed through an enhanced Hubble filter."

I couldn't reach out and touch it, but I could look and look. I'd read so much about this system. It was one of the few systems that was actually changing now: a binary system made up of one superbright star that might have been unstable, and one smaller star that orbited with it every five years. The two of them sat amidst large clouds of dust, and in the nineteenth century had made up the brightest star in the sky.

Since then, they had peaked and started to dim, and long before I was born, they ceased to be visible to the human eye. The fascination everyone had over them was the timescale of these changes. They were happening now, during human lifetimes. And in space, that's a rarity.

"Anything interesting going on?" I asked, watching those two shapes with a strange longing. Despite their huge differences, they'd been bound to each other for millions of years, neither ever making it outside the other one's gravity. In the loneliness of space, they were companionship, somehow.

"Possibly," Brandon said, with that smug smile. "We're looking at their mass. We had the Large Magellan trained on them a few weeks ago and there were indications of an alteration in mass and brightness since our last observation."

"Really?"

That was more than exciting. It was almost, possibly, a little scary. Because changes meant there might be a supernova. Stars like Eta Carinae burned brightly, but never for long. And if they went supernova, there would be effects we could actually feel. An increase in radiation to the point of harm was unlikely, but not impossible if the supernova kicked out enough energy. I remembered someone saying once that even if the atmosphere absorbed all of the radiation, there would be light enough from them for us to read at night.

"Looks like it, but we have to check," he said. "That's what I'll be running tonight."

I watched the two of them, trying, absurdly, to spot any signs of change in that beautiful twin star. As a teenager, I'd been excited about the thought of a supernova this close and soon. I'd willed something to happen to these two stars. But now, watching them, I felt nothing but sadness. They were going to blast apart from each other, and one of them probably wasn't going to survive.

Loco went to squeeze my hand again, picking up on something I think. I squeezed it back, but then I moved away from him with a heavy feeling.

"Thanks so much, Brandon, Axel. We'd better go and get on with boring life."

And I led the way outside.

14

ERRATIC ORBITS

Loco caught me up just outside the door, and drew gently on my arm until I stopped and faced him.
"Hey. What's up?"
"Dumb stuff," I said, with a half-smile.
"I was guessing that," he said, "given it's probably in connection with me…"

He closed in on me, filling me with the deliciousness of proximity and a scent of him. It was clear even though we were outside in a windy, slightly damp night. I wrapped my arms around his waist and drew him in to a hug.

"That was your cue to explain, Ms. Taylor," he muttered into my ear.

"I loved the stars," I said, not moving from that position. "It was pretty much my favourite first date ever, despite including two other people."

He laughed, gently. "But?"

"I've been watching those two stars for years," I said. "I mean, online, in videos and pictures. They're kind-of a pure symbol of partnership to me. I guess if you take the people out of the equation, it's easier for me to believe in a happily-ever-after."

"So these two stars which orbit round and round each other became a symbol, because they were strong enough to stay together for millions of years?"

"Pretty much," I agreed.

"And now it looks like they're going to destroy each other," he said, and moved his lips to chew my ear ever so gently. It was spine-tingling, arousing, and intensely distracting.

"Well, more accurately," I said, trying to concentrate, "one of them is going to brighten and become unstable, and then blast the other one out of existence, resulting in a spectacular but ultimately hollow remnant."

Loco paused in the ear-chewing, and then murmured, "My bet is on you to go unstable first. So I think you're safe. I mean, it's pretty obvious you're brighter than I am."

"You know, I'm not actually sure about that," I said, unable to fight his logic, or his desire, or my incandescent desire for him, either.

The kiss I gave him next wasn't an outdoor kind of a kiss; it was unmistakably a behind-doors, under-sheets, bedroom kind of a kiss that left us both breathless and reaching for more and more of each other.

He looked away briefly, towards the observatory, and then back at me. "Axel's going to be a while. My place?"

ONCE IT WAS DECIDED, and we were driving further East through Cambridge, it was suddenly difficult to break the space between us and touch him. There was so much desire in that car that you could practically hear it, but neither of us seemed able to interrupt it.

Loco drove us beyond the area of the city I knew well, and then onto memorial avenue and right out of anywhere I'd been. I knew that the Tobin Bridge led to the city of Chelsea, and that the city was essentially a collection of the more industrial buildings and businesses that made up the Boston-Cambridge conurbation. But that was about it.

It turned out to be a busy, square-built, not-very-green land just over the river. It swallowed us up in its grid of streets, until Loco pulled over at a row of houses opposite a disused warehouse. The one we'd stopped outside looked the best of the bunch, with an evergreen creeper grown half across it and signs of the bare limbs of others across the rest.

Loco was out of the car before I had time to say anything, and I followed with legs that shook a little and an overwhelming sense of urgency that was drowning out all my good sense. I do have some, you know. As much as it probably doesn't look like it.

He drew me past the main stone steps and onto a wrought-iron spiral staircase that wound up outside the building. It wasn't the climb that made my heart audible in my ears.

We were in the dimness of the small apartment at the top of the stairs before I was quite ready. We still weren't speaking, and Loco seemed to be as tense as I was as he flicked on a single light and showed a tiny, square hallway and a dim living-area beyond the one open door.

My hand was shaking where he took hold of it and drew me on further, through a closed door and into a room that smelled entirely of him. It was sparse and a little strewn with sports-clothes, but also cram-full of books and dominated by a poster of the Earth viewed from space.

That surprised me. I'd been subconsciously expecting football flags and memorabilia, and maybe some trophies. You don't get to be a scholarship student without winning a few on the way.

He let go of my hand for a moment to switch on what looked like a pretty clapped-out sound system. But when it came to life, it was a soft, lilting song which was only enhanced by the slight crackle of the speakers.

And then I forgot about the room and the music as Loco slowly peeled off his shirt, and then came towards me.

I met him halfway. The kiss that marked the point where we touched was so warm it made me shiver. I sank into it, knowing I shouldn't, and knowing that I was going to anyway.

Just tonight, I told myself. *Just tonight. I'll be strong in the morning.*

The heat of his body started to seep into me, too, and I began shrugging off my fitted wool sweater, trying not to break the kiss as I did it. Loco's hands came up under it, too, and I let him break away for a moment as he pulled it over my head. It caught under my ear for a moment, and then came free in what I knew was a cloud of hair-frizzing static, but it was hard to care at all about that.

I slid my hands inside the waistband of his jeans, our mouths together again and growing softer with wetness. His fingers sent constant shivers up me as he lifted my top achingly slowly. Once it had cleared my carefully-chosen lacy bra, he ended the kiss to lean down and kiss me along the line of my collar bone, one soft, light kiss at a time. He followed the line of my neck upwards and I moved my hands to twist them in his hair.

He unhooked the bra for me, after only a few failed attempts that made me smile. He was still making those slow lines of kisses on my skin, an agonisingly sweet touch.

I let my hands snake down his back, and then drew them around to where I could feel the hardness of him pressing into me. I slid his belt off and in a slightly clumsy move, pulled his pants downwards until he was free of them and that erection of his banged into my stomach.

I could hear his breathing grow faster as I pulled his underwear clear too. And then I wanted to see him, to look at him, and I drew back and ran my eyes over the flesh-and-muscle lines of him. Oh jeez, was he hot. I wanted him inside me with an ache I almost couldn't stand.

He stooped to remove the pants and underwear - and also, with a brief smile, his sneakers and socks.

When he touched me again, it was to run his hands up my stomach until he was touching my breasts from below. With a light touch, he used the thumb of each hand to stroke briefly across my nipples, and I felt such a strength of reaction deep in my groin that I grabbed him and pulled him into another mouth-on-mouth kiss.

He lifted me up and moved me to sit on the edge of the bed, still kissing me whilst he drew off first my knee-high boots, then my cashmere stockings, and finally the clingy black skirt I'd worn for exactly this situation. It slid off and left me finally as naked as he was.

Loco moved his mouth down to my breasts and sucked at first one then the other while I folded my legs around him and tried not to moan out loud.

"You know something?" he murmured, between kisses that began drawing up towards my jaw.

"What?" I whispered back.

"Just like this, just now, you - are - perfect. Absolutely - totally - perfect."

I could feel my eyes overflowing slightly as I drew him back into a kiss again, and then over me as I leaned back onto the bed. He paused for a moment to pull open a drawer next to the bed, and I watched with a smile as he tore open a blue condom-wrapper.

"And right now, so are you," I whispered back.

A few seconds later, he had slid inside me. And in spite of knowing that I shouldn't have been doing it, knowing that this was still the worst of all bad ideas, it felt like I'd finally found the other half of myself.

15

TIES

I'd expected to feel stupid, and wretched, and to want to run from him. It wouldn't have been the first time. When I'd first slept with Brad, a month into our relationship, I'd had exactly that reaction and had to pretend I'd forgotten about a tutorial in order to leave without hurting his feelings. And that had been after a month, not after the overwhelming lack of self control of going home with Loco after a first proper date.

But instead of feeling stupid, I felt peaceful lying against him as the sweat slowly cooled on me and he moved his hand up and down my back in erratic patterns. The incredibly slow thud of his heart was soothing, and just then, I didn't believe in it all ending disastrously.

Which didn't stop the note of melancholy that lay behind the calm, but it at least let me enjoy it.

"What are you thinking?" he asked me, after we'd lain in silence for a while.

"That this is actually quite nice," I said, a little bit wryly.

"You know what'd make it nicer?" he asked.

"What?"

"If you stroked my hair for me while I dribbled onto the pillow."

I laughed at him, but we shifted and I did it anyway, watching his face while he lay with his eyes closed.

"You aren't going to run out on me in a minute, are you?" he asked, sleepily.

"Wasn't planning on it," I said. "Which is worrying."

He reached out and squeezed my leg, with a grin, and then was quiet for a few minutes.

"You want to get some food in a while?"

It hadn't occurred to me to be hungry yet, but I realised that I was.

"What time is it?"

Loco reached his other arm out, eyes still closed, and batted it around until he found his cell-phone on the dresser. He squinted at it. "Almost nine."

"OK, so it's acceptable to say that I'm *starving*."

"Cally, it is *always* acceptable to say that you're starving," he answered, and then added, "What are we doing tomorrow?"

I couldn't help smiling at that. It didn't matter that I'd promised myself this was just for today. And then I sighed, realising that there was going to be a really big coding project waiting for me in the IT lab.

"I'm probably going to have my feedback on my project back, which means I'm going to have to work pretty much all day."

"Yup, good," he said, "so I was thinking we could take a boat out on the river."

I laughed. "I really do have to work. We could do something in the evening, though. Once my eyes are really red and I look like I haven't been outside enough."

"OK, evening it is," he said, and drew me down to lie next to him again. He wrapped himself over me, and kissed my ear. It made me shiver all over again. "I guess I'll just have to hang out in the lab and do my very important ear-chewing work during the day."

I turned to kiss him on the mouth instead.

"You know, you're kind-of cute after sex," I told him. "It's a little bit pathetic. What happened to the big manly footballer?"

"I think he went the same way as the prickly, mean, get-your-hands-off-me mathmo," he answered, giving me a look out of those green eyes. "But it's ok. I won't tell anyone. And in public, you can walk along in front of me and I'll carry all your things and say, 'Yes, Cally,' to everything you ask of me."

"But it's no fun if you don't argue," I complained.

The calm was gradually ebbing away, but not in favour of any fear or recriminations on the part of my conscience. It was being pushed out of the way by a renewal of the same desire that had brought me here, and I could see it rising up again in him, too.

I moved my hips forwards so that our bodies were against each other, and then slid down a little. Loco responded by pushing against my shoulder a little roughly, and then kissing me hotly.

It took us another hour to get out of the apartment.

WE MADE WERE both a little flushed and glassy-eyed by the time we made it to an Italian restaurant a few blocks away. Loco clearly came here often, as the fifty-something owner greeted him as Luca and chatted to him for a while about football results. The place was small and tatty, but the food, when it came, was incredible, and the kind of thing you might actually get in Italy instead of the Americanised version of it.

We started to talk more after we'd demolished a platter of freshly-baked bread with oil and some huge, soft olives. Loco wanted to know more about Fernando and my Mom, so I ended up telling him the full story of my parents and then how it had all changed.

"My Dad was visiting the UK when they met," I said. "He proposed to my Mom the same day, and she was totally smitten. Enough to move away from her home and come to live here."

"She's British?" he asked.

"Yeah. She was born in Bristol."

Loco nodded.

"What happened to your Dad?" he asked.

"Bowel cancer," I said, as briefly as I could. "It wasn't diagnosed for a long time, and it had spread to his lungs and his liver. It was... short, and vicious. It tore my Mom to pieces."

"I'm sorry," he said.

"I know," I said, smiling at him.

"Didn't your Mom want to move home?" he asked.

I shook my head. "I don't think she could face leaving everything that reminded her of him. And I think she worried about disrupting me when I was settled at school. But actually, I was just heartsick for my Dad and for her."

"And that was the first time you made anyone fall in love," he said, giving me his focused green gaze. It was so strange talking about this to someone who was so genuinely interested, and who didn't think I was making it up.

"Yeah," I said. "I actually knew Fernando a little. My Mom was manager of the bar in this hotel. The kind of place you get a lot of businessmen. Sometimes she'd have to have me there because she couldn't afford childcare, and Fernando was there one evening and saw me hiding out behind the bar, playing with putty. My mom was nowhere nearby, and he was nice to me. Really kind. I just... I wished my Mom could have someone like him so I could have a Dad again and she could be happy. I wished it so hard, and then I started feeling it happening. My Mom walked back over to the bar and it was...

it was just like it always is. They just locked on to each other, and that was it."

"And you knew you'd done it?"

"Yeah," I said, trying to remember how I'd felt. "I don't think I was sure, but something had happened."

"And they lived happily ever after," he said, smiling.

"They did," I said, and then added, "Did I mention Fernando is filthy rich?"

Our plates of pasta arrived in the hands of the owner, and the way he paused and looked at me with a smile made it obvious he was looking for an introduction.

"This is Cally, Alfeo," Loco said.

"Delighted," Alfeo said, taking my hand in his dry, rough palms for a second. "I hope you enjoy your food?"

"It's delicious so far," I said, enthusiastically. "Really, really good."

"I'm glad." He turned back to Loco. "I'll let Rita take over in a few moments. She'll be happy to see you back."

"They like you, don't they?" I muttered to Loco.

"I've tried telling them I'm an asshole," he said. "But I guess I keep buying too much pasta to make them hate me. And I bring Axel in, too, and naturally, they adore him."

"I'm not surprised," I said, thinking of his brother's absolute good-looks.

"You liked him too, didn't you?"

"Yeah," I said. "I liked him a lot. It's hard not to like that kind of enthusiasm."

"What did you think of Brandon?" Loco asked, and I could tell it was a loaded question.

"I thought," I said, slowly, remembering Brandon's apparent indifference to his boyfriend, "that Axel could do a lot better."

Loco nodded, thoughtfully, and then said, "I agree. But I'm... The thing with Axel is, he's easily swayed. He wants to make everyone like him, and that makes him pretty vulnerable. For one thing, he always goes for people he has to chase hard, which seems dumb when he has a lot of guys falling at his feet. And he's only seventeen. It's not like he *needs* to be with someone."

"So," I said, thinking about this, "Brandon is a lot better than some of the alternatives?"

"Exactly," Loco said.

"You said before that you'd moved back to try and help him out somehow," I asked, curious but trying not to pry too hard. "Was it to do with that?"

"Yes and no," he said, and looked like he was about to continue when the kitchen door opened and a really beautiful girl walked through it. She was dressed in a pencil skirt and tight white blouse, but it fit her like a ball-gown and only seemed to bring out her glossy dark hair and full lips.

Her face lit up as she saw Loco.

"Luca, what are you doing back here?"

She stalked over to him, armed with a pencil and a notebook. I might as well not have existed for all the notice she gave me.

"Hey Rita," he said, standing. "Good to see you."

Loco gave her a hug while she beamed, and I could have torn the both of them to pieces right then.

"You're back for good?" she asked, drawing a strand of hair out of her eyes.

"Well, at least till I'm through with the scholarship," Loco answered.

"You got any games coming up? Papa and I would love to come and support."

"Oh, yeah," he said, sitting back down but still smiling. "Next weekend. Hey, maybe you guys can hook up with Cally."

Rita looked at me, then, still smiling but with a little air of wariness. It didn't surprise me. She clearly adored him, and I couldn't actually blame her for it.

Obviously, I still hated her.

"Yeah," she rallied. "That would be nice."

By the time she'd left, I had no appetite at all. Not even for the most delicious plate of tagliatelli.

I felt sick, and shaky. I could tell myself to stop being jealous as much as I wanted, but it didn't stop the fact that this was how it was going to be in the end. My worst fears were going to come true, because there was nothing I could do to stop them. I was going to lose him, and it was going to tear me to pieces.

Loco was talking to me, but I couldn't even hear him. All I could feel was my heart pounding in my ears.

"Are you ok?" he asked, loudly enough that it broke through the roar.

"I have to get out," I said. "I'm sorry. I'm sorry. I can't."

And I ran, out into a neighbourhood I didn't know, ignoring him as he called after me and trying to ignore the tears that were overtaking me, too.

16

THE FEAR AT MY BACK

I don't know to this day whether running was the stupidest thing I'd done in days, or the most sensible. That part of Chelsea was not a good area to be alone in late at night. I could feel it as I got out there onto the street. There were cars pulled up against the sidewalk with conversations happening in and around them, and as I ran past the first one, a young guy in leathers and converse gave me a long, level stare.

I realised that I was drawing more attention to myself by running. I slowed down, after a glance behind me showed that Loco wasn't running after me. Not yet, at least. I knew the bridge back over to Boston was somewhere in this direction. I just had to walk.

I tried to breathe, and to look casual, like I was always out here late at night. But I found myself death-gripping my shoulder-bag, and flinching every time there was a sound.

When I heard hurrying footsteps behind me a short while later, fear coursed through me. I glanced behind me, and saw not Loco but a teenager, hooded and stony-eyed. He flicked his eyes to the ground and I sped up.

Just ahead of me, a car slid past and then slowed and started to pull in. The window came down and a guy leaned out of the passenger window, his eyes hazy and a half-smile on his face . I sped up again as he called out, "What you doing, lady?"

I ignored him, but the car started to move with me as I drew level, matching my pace.

"Why aren't you dressed up?" he asked, and a girl leaned out of the back to laugh.

"You dress like my Mom," she said, and I glanced at her inches-thick make-up and her curled lip and I started feeling pissed off. They were just bored, and had seen someone looking vulnerable. I couldn't understand that decision to make someone else's life harder for no good reason.

"Want to take some fashion advice from her?" I snapped back, and then smiled, as I kept hurrying.

"No, I don't," she said, and then was cut across, by the guy in the passenger seat saying, "You should be ashamed of yourself, you look awful."

"Awww, you are just the cutest," I told him, wondering how long I was going to have to put up with this. Though at least they might make it less likely that the guy behind me tried to rob me. I glanced over my shoulder, and he was pretty close behind.

The car sped up slightly, but instead of overtaking, the driver pulled it into a driveway ahead of me and blocked my way. A little bit of fear came back. Maybe the guy behind was part of this, and I had nowhere to go.

I started trying to step round the back of the car, but the guy reversed and I had to stop for fear of being run down.

"We're trying to give you some help," the passenger said. "You should be grateful."

I heard a few jogging footsteps and flinched.

"Hey," the teenager said. "Leave the lady alone."

Very gently, he took my arm and walked around the back of

the car. They made no move, apparently outnumbered by two. Until we were right behind them, that is.

If I hadn't jumped forwards, I would have been hit. There was no question. The kid had to stop me falling, because I'd lunged so fast.

The car screamed backwards into the road, and the driver shouted "Ugly bitch!" at me, before slamming on the breaks, and forcing the protesting car to go forwards instead.

I started babbling at the teenage guy, shaken and stunned. I was trying to thank him, and was in the middle of making no sense whatever when I felt a strange hot sensation pressing at me. I stopped talking and watched numbly as the driver of that car over-corrected for the curve as he'd started and lost control. Only a couple of hundred metres down the road, the car smashed into a lamp-post. The bumper crumpled and the tail swung out into the road before coming to a stop.

I looked behind me, my skin crawling, for the source of the heat, and I saw Loco not far away, his chest moving rapidly and his hands in fists by his sides.

I DIDN'T crawl into bed until almost three. Loco hadn't tried to talk to me again. Maybe he'd seen the horror on my face, or maybe he hadn't wanted to have any involvement while the three idiots in the car sorted out the mess. He'd turned and walked away, off into the night somewhere.

"Total morons," the teenager said, shaking his head. And then, "You want me to walk you anywhere?"

I was watching the three of them scrambling out of the car, inspecting the damage. I was waiting to see injuries, though they seemed to be ok.

"Do you think we ought to help?" I asked.

The kid laughed. "They deserved it."

"Did they?" I whispered.

He walked me further up the road, and then flagged down a cab for me. Despite my thoughts on him and his hooded sweater and his cold expression, he turned out to be kind. Which is yet another example in my life of judging too quickly. He even asked me if I needed him to pay.

"No, no," I said, quickly, trying to smile at him. "I've got enough money with me. I should probably be paying you for rescuing me."

He looked almost annoyed for a second. "I don't need paying," he said, and he shut the door, nodded, and walked away.

The cab-driver was a little bit too talkative for my mood just then, but his chatter gradually soothed me. He was Italian, and I wondered if he knew Alfeo and Rita. Despite what had just happened, the thought of her with Loco still gave me that rush of nausea and jealousy. To my shame, it was worse than the horror I'd felt at the crash.

I lay thinking about it for the few minutes I managed to stay awake, imagining Rita with her arms around him; Rita kissing him; Rita giving me a sympathetic grin as he pulled her towards him. As my thoughts grew more confused, I saw the two of them getting married, and imagined having to be their bridesmaid while a procession of my lost friends and exes stood in the audience.

But perhaps my subconscious has more sense. When I slept, it was to dream that Loco was calling down awful black-feathered, crow-like creatures to peck at me and slice me with their wings, and that on some level I deserved it.

CAMPUS WAS ALMOST DESERTED that Monday morning. Most of the students had left for home over the weekend, free of the coding project and the work ethic that plagued me. I passed by a lot of stores that were fully gearing up for the festive season, but the weather had decided to do its own thing. It was a warm, bright day with a pale blue sky and a taste of late summer about it.

It didn't suit my mood much, either.

I was doing what I'd always done when I lost someone. I was holding it together by working. I was well practiced at hardening myself, and pretending that nothing was wrong until it had gotten easier.

Several times on the bike ride over there, my mind had drifted onto thoughts of Loco being angry with me, and what that might mean. But whenever it did, I told myself that was another good reason to disentangle myself now. And I tried to suppress the squeeze in my stomach at the idea of letting him go; to forget the recent, oh-so-sexy feel of him; to block out thoughts of him poised over me, my legs wrapped around him and our mouths hotly pressed together.

When I heard a text arrive on my cellphone as I was locking up my bike, I made myself ignore it while I pulled my chain and my d-lock out, found my keys and attached them both. I kept on ignoring it while I took my helmet off and put my keys away, and only reached into my jacket pocket once I'd reflected that it might be from my Mom, needing something.

I knew it wasn't from her, but sometimes it's easier to kid yourself.

WILL you come and have coffee with me this morning? x

RIGHT THEN, I hated the way my heart squeezed, and the instant lift in my mood. I hated them, because they were both part of a weakness I couldn't afford.

I closed the message, and was putting my phone away again when I realised that ignoring him was just cruel. I had to tell him no, firmly but calmly.

I HAVE TO WORK, Loco. And I know it's a bad idea. I'm sorry. x

HIS NEXT TEXT arrived before I was even through the door of the computer lab.

BAD IDEAS SEEM to appeal to you, though. Are you sure I can't persuade you? I think talking through a few things would be pretty sensible. x

I COULD FEEL THOSE AWFUL, pathetic tears pricking my eyes. He was right. It would be sensible. Talking about things always helped me get perspective, and reason things out; in every part of my life except this one.

I KNOW. But I also know that I can't do it, Loco. I'm so sorry.

I TURNED my phone off after that, and went to the furthest corner of the upstairs lab to hide from him. It took a whole can of diet coke to swallow down the thick lump in my throat.

HIDING TURNED out not to work that well in the end. As I exited the building at lunchtime to head for the cafeteria (not the one at the Sports' Centre, just in case) I saw Loco crossing the square slowly, his hands in his football-jacket pockets and his face distant. He faltered when he saw me, which was one up on me. I stopped moving entirely, socked in the stomach all over again by how hot he was.

He moved slowly over to me, hesitantly, watching my face for a reaction.

"Come on," he said, once he was a few paces away. "Just a quick talk. Somewhere quiet."

For probably the tenth time, I gave in to him. I felt like I owed it to him, but maybe that was just a justification for something I wanted to do.

We found a secluded spot on the sunny side of one of the large trees outside the science and technology building. A few other students had had the same idea, but were dispersed over the lawn. None of them were within earshot, or that easily within sight.

"Why did you run?" he asked me, looking out at the open space instead of at me.

"Because I realised it was only going to end badly. I could see it, and I'm not willing to go through it."

He nodded, and then said, "I don't see how you can know that."

"Loco," I said, a little exasperated. "There's no way it can end any other way. What I do is bound to happen, and then... it's worse than that with you."

"Because of what I do?" he asked, looking at me expressionlessly. "Because you think I'm going to get angry and have some kind of revenge on you?"

"You did get angry," I said, feeling my heart speed up. It was half the memory of the crash he'd caused and half an unwanted memory of the couple of hours we'd spent in his room. "I saw the results."

"Yes, I did," he said, beginning to sound a little frustrated. "I did get angry. And you want to know why?"

He seemed to be waiting for an answer, so I shrugged.

"I got angry because it's not so different from what I do, and I've learned to control it. I got angry because you're not willing to give that a chance. I got angry because you don't seem to trust me to have any choice over who I fall in love with. And then I got angrier because someone tried to run you down with their car."

And he really sounded angry now. I put a hand onto his arm, trying to calm him, and then I drew it away again as I realised I couldn't touch him any more.

"But you didn't control it," I said. "I don't blame you for it, but you didn't control it. I saw what happened, and I felt it. That car crashed because of you."

"You think that wasn't controlling it?" he asked, half angry, but half simply disbelieving. "Do you have any idea what I could have done to them? For trying to hurt you for no reason at all, and for hurling spite at you because it was better than being bored? I could have destroyed them, Cally. And I didn't. I could have hurt you, too, but I am never, ever going to want to do that. It doesn't matter what you do, or what you say."

He was so close to me that I was breathing in the warm air from his mouth. It was dizzying, and wonderful. It would have been so easy just to lean in and kiss him. But even if he was right about the anger, and right about his control over it, it wasn't the same for me. The only way of control was what I was already doing: not getting close to someone.

"I don't think you'll hurt me," I said quietly, nodding. "But that doesn't change anything."

He gave a disgusted noise, and drew away a little. "Stop doing that," he said.

"Stop doing what?"

"Putting all your defences up," he said. "Retreating. I'm not going to take it lying down. I've seen too much of the real you. I know it's not true. You aren't cold or hard or tough. You're hiding everything you really are, and turning your back on the real thing."

"The real thing?" I asked, trying to raise an eyebrow at me with my usual sarcasm while my heart was in my throat.

"You can lie to a lot of people," he said, in a low, slightly hoarse voice, "but I know how you feel about me. You love me as much as I love you."

It knocked me for six. It's humiliating to admit it, but it left me wanting nothing more than to fold into him and kiss him and kiss him. I'd always been pretty voluble about how stupid it is to declare love for someone before you've been dating for a while, but here the words were, out in the open, and they made me feel weak and dizzy with happiness.

Weak, the more rational part of me chipped in. *You don't get to be weak.*

It took all the self control I could manage to stand up, and move away a step. I had to stop this. I had to stop it now, to be fair on both of us.

"I don't love you," I said. It didn't sound like me, that cold tone belied by a shake in my voice and in my body. "I've realised that I hate you."

I turned away from him, some part of me crumpling with the hurt of me whilst another was nothing but relieved.

"How much?" I heard him call.

"What?"

I shouldn't have looked back, but he was on his feet and asking me again, his face calm and a little half-smile on his lips.

"How much do you hate me? Just a little bit? Or a lot. Do you really, really hate me?"

He was moving closer to me, and I folded my arms over my chest, trying to stop the shaking. "A lot," I said, as firmly as I could. "Totally. I... I hate you so much that I never want to see you again. It's so - it's so strong that I can't think about anything else, and it's getting in the way of my life." He was closer, and nodding, and somehow it was encouraging me to go on. "I just - I hate you so much that I sometimes can't sleep for thinking about it. It's like I need more time in my day for how much - for how much I..."

I knew as I felt my arms go around his back, and our lips and our tongues lock together in a ferocious kiss that this was it: I had no more resistance to offer. I'd tried to do the right thing; I'd tried and I'd tried. But sometimes there just isn't any more fight left.

17

BINARY

I wasn't going to achieve much work for the rest of the day. Loco actually offered to keep himself occupied while I worked, but the effect of all the sadness, lust, happiness, anxiety and resignation that had thundered through me was a wasted, empty feeling.

"What do you want to do?" he asked me quietly, lying with an arm over me on the grass. "We could bike somewhere, drive somewhere, walk somewhere..."

"I don't think I have the get-up-and-go for biking," I admitted. "I'm feeling kind of nuked."

"That's good, cos I'm supposed to be taking a rest day," he said, with a grin. "So what about a movie, and some dinner, and then an early night?"

"That sounds pretty amazing," I muttered, turning on my back to look at the very deep blue overhead. "You'll have to let me pay, this time. And maybe we should... not go to that Italian again."

He laughed. "It's ok. Alfeo wasn't offended. He thought I'd said something to offend you. And Rita thought it was her fault."

"Well," I admitted, feeling heat in my face, "it sort-of was her fault."

"Really?" He sounded surprised. Not quite as emotionally-aware as I'd thought, then. Or maybe he was just being polite.

"Not her, exactly," I added. "More what she represented."

"Oh." It didn't sound like he'd had a revelation about it, so I turned onto my elbow to talk directly to him.

"You know what I mean?"

"Not really." He gave me such a relaxed grin that it made me smile.

"She's obviously into you in a big way," I told him, and shushed him when he tried to protest. "She is. It's not difficult to tell. And I saw her, and imagined how it would feel if you reciprocated, and I hated it. Just... hated it. And given that it's pretty inevitable, I knew I had to get out."

"It's not inevitable," he said, giving me a steady look. "If I can control what I do, then so can you."

"I don't think it's that simple," I said, a little irritably. I wanted him to be right, but this was my particular cross to bear in life. I hated the idea that he'd just been tougher at handling his strange ability. "How do you control yours?"

"I keep my temper," he said. "I don't let myself hate. It usually involves seeing all the good things in someone, no matter what they've done, or all the human things. If it's really hard, I imagine how I'd feel if something awful happened to my brother, and I stop myself that way."

"Yeah," I said, nodding, "which is the problem. I can't not care about people. That's what I've spent my life trying to do, and it leaves you alone. I can't be in a relationship with someone without caring about them, obviously. I can't not care about you."

"So it has to be done another way," he said, shrugging. "I

mean, what about working out how to make it happen for yourself?"

"I've tried," I said, trying not to be grouchy. He was trying to help me; to help us. "I've thought about it, about how much I want someone to come along and for us to just...connect like that. I mean, I was a heart-broken teenage girl like everyone else. I tried it a lot. But nothing happened."

He nodded, thinking, then said, "It happens when you come to care about someone, right? So... maybe you need to learn to love yourself a little more."

I met his gaze, nodded slowly, and then said, "You know, that's the biggest load of self-help crap I've ever heard."

He grinned. "I kept a straight face, though."

"You did. Well done. But if you really believe that, we might not be able to date."

He gave me a light kiss on the lips. "Really? Because it might have a point to it. Maybe instead of focusing on what you want, you need to focus on why you deserve it."

"I know," I said, sighing. "And I have. I really, truly have. I don't think changing my attitude is going to solve this one."

"OK," he said, with another one of those shrugs. "So solution No. 1 doesn't work. Which means you're going to have to train yourself to control it even when you like someone."

"You want to tell me how I'm going to do that?" I asked him.

"Pick someone," he said, "someone you're going to see fairly regularly. And concentrate on all the things that are great about them, and how much they deserve someone special. And then, when you start feeling it happen, try and stop that feeling. Not the caring about them; just the feeling of it happening."

"Hmm," I said, doubtfully. "I'm pretty sure I try and stop it whenever I lose a best friend."

"So that's why you need to do it with someone you're less close to," he argued, sitting up. "When it's your best friend, or your boyfriend, it's going to be really strong, and hard to disentangle the two feelings from each other, and from all your hurt at losing them. Pick someone you don't mind losing."

"You have someone in mind?" I asked him, narrowing my eyes at him.

"The perfect person," he said, grinning.

"Oh." It was obvious, really. "Axel."

"You said yourself that he deserves better," Loco said, lifting my hand up and kissing it absently. "And if it goes wrong, it'll be the best thing that happened to him. No more Brandons. And no more much worse guys."

"How much worse?"

He sighed. "A lot worse. His last boyfriend, Rhett, was a drug-dealer, who tried his hardest to get Axel hooked on cocaine."

"Oh."

"Yup," he said. "So it's not a problem if you fail. It's ideal. You liked him, and you'll see him off and on if you don't run out on me again."

"I'm not running out on you again," I said, with certainty. "There are times when you can run, and other times when you just have to hold on and close your eyes."

He laughed, a gradually growing laugh.

"What?" I asked.

"I just... I just really wanted to say, 'That's what you get when you ride the Loco coaster.' But I just couldn't do it deadpan."

I shook my head with a sigh. "It's ok. I think I've had as much of your deadpan as I can take just now."

I was grinning as he helped me to my feet. I kissed him hotly on the mouth again, the world seeming strangely soft as I did it. Love is such a strange thing.

. . .

The Cupid Touch

I LOVED THE FILM. We managed to find a futuristic sci-fi dystopia with lots of space travel, and it turned out to be absolutely Loco's thing too. In the usual way of things, it would have boded well for the future, as would have the way we kept in physical contact with each other the whole way through the film. I felt so comfortable with him, and I kept getting surges of pride that he was mine every time I looked at him. It was like being a teenager, without all the bitterness I remembered from knowing I could never keep anyone.

Once it had finished, Loco looped his arm through mine, and said, "So I was thinking a takeaway. We can eat it at my place."

I looked at him, slightly suspicious. "Are you trying to get me to hang out with Axel so I can practice?"

"Well ultimately, maybe," he answered. "But in the short term, he has a shift tonight and shouldn't be back until midnight. I thought we should take advantage of some peace."

"Not arguing," I said, moving my arm so that it was around his waist. It was impossible not to remember how it had been the last time we'd been in that apartment. I wondered if we really needed to get takeout first, but Loco seemed to be fixed on it.

"OK, deal-breaker question," he said, as we spilled out onto the street. "Chinese, Indian or Thai?"

"Well I could eat any of them," I answered. "But I'll think less of you if you don't like Thai."

"Ohhh, right answer," he said, squeezing me. "That's good. We can continue to date."

"Such a relief," I said, sarcastically.

IT TURNED out waiting for takeout with Loco was almost as good as watching the film. He started telling me about his natural talent for embarrassing himself. I couldn't imagine him ever being embarrassed about anything, and his stories only convinced me more. He laughed over every slip-up or mistake, and I wished I could feel more like that about screwing up.

The guy taking orders behind the counter was listening to his stories, too, and laughing almost as much as I was.

"I had this thing a while after I passed my driving test," he told me. "You know how you feel pretty good about yourself once you're no longer learning? I couldn't park for shit, but I felt pretty good if I ended up with my car not-actually-in-the-road. So anyway, I'd parked really badly on a narrow street and jogged into a hardware store to pick something up. I'd just paid when I heard someone blasting on their horn. I went out, and there was a learner driver with an instructor's car, totally unable to get past. I was annoyed about it, because I figured there was still a load of room."

"Was there actually?" I asked.

"Other cars had got past," he said. "But admittedly, it was pretty tight. Anyway, I basically stormed out of the store, looking straight at this poor kid in the car, doing my big intimidating guy thing. Because I was always a big guy, you know? I was this size at sixteen. So there I was, making the most of it. I stalked round the car and got in, slammed the door - and then realised I'd gotten in the passenger side."

I was laughing so hard I was on the verge of snorting. "You total idiot!"

"I was used to getting in the passenger side," he protested, grinning.

"What'd you do?"

"I did the only thing a self-respecting arrogant teenager can do," he said. "I stared at the guy as I got out of the car, and held his gaze the whole way around so that neither him or the instructor could laugh. And then I got in the right side and stalled just before I drove off."

"That's a total train-wreck," I said, shaking my head. "It's no wonder you ended up so shy."

Our order arrived on the counter and we took it the few blocks to Loco's house.

"I think it's your turn with an embarrassing story," Loco said, a little way on.

"Ah, I don't have any," I said, shaking my head. "I'm just too utterly cool for that kind of thing."

"Really?" he asked.

"Yup. I was born in control of my look. It never slips."

"OK," he said, nodding. "So it won't matter if I do this..."

He moved in a lurch, picking me up and swinging me over his shoulder in a fireman's carry.

"No!" I screeched. "Put me down, you idiot."

Instead, he started jogging, and I was growling complaints at him for the couple of minutes it took to get to his apartment block, whilst trying not to laugh.

We were both breathless by the time he'd carried me up the stairs and deposited me at the top.

"You have some seriously good thighs on you," I said, as he pulled out his keys and unlocked the door.

He was gearing up to say something in return when the door swung open and the sound of voices reached us. I saw the way Loco's face changed, from fun to concerned, and then to anger with a hint of that danger I'd seen in him from the start.

"Shit," I heard him say, quietly, as Axel swung into view from the kitchen and then stopped short.

I saw the way Axel's face changed too, and it disturbed me a lot. It was like someone had sucked all the colour out of him. A small, dapper guy appeared behind him, his eyes immediately going towards Loco. He smiled, a predatory kind of smile.

"Ah, Luca. Nice to see you again."

I glanced at Loco's hand, which was still holding the key, and was clenched so tightly around it that his knuckles had gone white, and i wondered if I ought to just back away and get out of this whole situation. But I was in it with Loco now, for better or for the very-likely much worse. So instead, I took a step towards him and put my arm around his waist.

"Rhett," Loco said, in a soft voice. "Mind telling me what the hell you're doing here?"

18

A HISTORY OF DEPENDENCE

"How could you be so *stupid?*"

"It wasn't - you don't understand the kind of pressure there was when I was with those guys."

"Which is why I told you to ditch them all!"

Loco looked as if he wanted to put a fist through the wall. I could see him holding the anger in, controlling it. Axel still looked a little afraid, but I realised it wasn't because he thought Loco was going to punch him: he flinched every time his older brother spoke, hurt by the words and (I thought) by Loco's poor opinion.

Rhett had gone, to my great relief. There was something lizard-like about him, and within a few moments of meeting him I'd come to understand the intensity of Loco's dislike for his brother's short, well-dressed ex.

But he hadn't departed without leaving a little poison behind him. He'd answered Loco's question, but with a self-satisfied smile.

"It's a business visit, Luca. I'm here to make some arrangements with your brother following a slightly disappointing earlier transaction."

Loco's sharp glance at Axel, who looked totally wretched, was enough to tell me that this was really not good news.

"What transaction?" he asked his brother, but Rhett interrupted.

"Why don't we all have a seat and discuss it? I'd value your input, Luca."

Loco turned back to him, and for a fraction of a second, the smile on Rhett's face faltered.

"You don't invite me to sit in my own kitchen, Rhett. We'll discuss it here."

Rhett held up his hands, placating him.

"No disrespect intended."

"Tell me," Loco said, looking at Rhett this time.

"This dates back a while," Lizard Rhett said. "When we were... when the two of us were seeing each other, Axel was enthusiastic about becoming involved in business with me."

Axel's mouth went slack for a second, and I was pretty sure from his shock that there hadn't been a lot of enthusiasm.

"I gave him an opportunity," Rhett went on, leaning back against the doorframe and looking way too comfortable. "I needed someone to carry a package for me, and Axel seemed the right choice. But unfortunately, he let me down, which landed me in a rather difficult position with my employer."

Loco had gone very still, but I could feel tension running through him. I wanted to reassure him, but it wasn't the time. Not while Rhett was standing there, relaxed and smiling.

"So what did you do about it?"

"There wasn't a lot I could do," Rhett said, with a shrug. "It was awkward. It was a very valuable shipment that he lost."

"I didn't lose it," Axel interrupted, with surprising sharpness. "It was stolen from me."

"I'm not blaming you," Rhett said, with absolutely the fakest kindness. "But unfortunately it means that you owe a large sum of money to Mr. Jeroniri, and you've failed to come up with it for some time now."

"How much?" Loco asked, quietly.

"Eleven thousand," Rhett said, solemn for a moment. But I could see his mouth twitching with trying not to smile.

"Eleven thousand?" he asked, incredulous. "You gave a seventeen-year-old kid eleven grand of drugs and you think this is his fault?"

"It's not about fault," Rhett said, shifting a little uncomfortably. "It's about what he owes."

Loco shook his head. "If you're stupid enough to entrust something of that value to a kid who has no way of repaying it, you can take responsibility. Now get the fuck out of my house."

Rhett shook his head. "Now Luca, you don't want to do anything you might regret. Mr. Jeroniri is not someone you want to anger."

"And neither am I," Loco said, taking two very slow steps forwards so that I had to let go of him.

Rhett clearly didn't know how true this was. But the threat of his large presence was enough to make the smaller man take a step backwards.

"You're not understanding me," Rhett started to say, but then Loco closed on him.

I wasn't too sure what happened just after that. It was some kind of scuffle, but it was impossible to see beyond Loco's broad back. I could feel something, though. It was that hot, buzzing anger that came before Loco brought revenge down on someone.

"Don't, Loco!" I said, and it must have surprised him enough that the mood faltered.

Rhett twisted his way free of Loco and was suddenly running past me. I felt a little sick as I realised he was holding a knife.

"Stay away from my brother!" Loco yelled, turning to call after him.

The heat and the buzzing took a long time to ease. I came up to hug him, and despite the rage running through him, he sagged into the hug and clung onto me tightly.

"He isn't worth it, is he?" I asked him.

"No," he replied, into my ear. "No, he isn't."

And then Loco had let me go and rounded on his brother.

"I take it what he said was true, in the essentials," he said.

"I - yeah," Axel said, and then quickly added, "but it's not quite how it sounded. He pressured me about it for weeks, because the cops were apparently watching him and I didn't look like someone to arrest. I had to walk through a lot of really crappy places late at night with this bag over my shoulder, and some guys grabbed it and knocked me down before running."

Which was the point at which Loco had erupted at him.

"I did break it off with the in the end," Axel had eventually managed to say. "It was all that drug-mule shit that pushed me into it. I realised how nasty he could be, and I didn't like him any more."

"You should have told me," Loco said, a little more calmly.

"I didn't want to freak you out," Axel said, going to take a seat in the kitchen.

There was a silence, while Loco visibly took a tighter hold on his anger.

"Do you think he'll come back?" Axel asked, a little shake to his voice.

"I don't know," Loco replied. "I hope not."

He met my gaze then, and I could see what he was thinking. That there was always a solution if he did. I gave him an attempt at a smile.

"I guess he's going to be under pressure from Jeroniri," Axel said. "It's a real mess."

"And he needs a scape-goat, yeah," Loco said. "But he has that kind of money to waste. He's not going to end up screwed."

"You think he faked the theft?" I asked, tentatively. "To screw his boss over?"

They both looked up at me, sharply, and then I saw Loco thinking it through.

"I mean, it was never the best idea, using a seventeen-year-old," I went on. "And it's awful convenient that you happened to get robbed of that bag. They didn't stop to take anything else, right? Even though there were a few of them and only one of you?"

Axel shook his head, slowly, and then suddenly exclaimed, "The slimy fucker! How could he do that?"

"Because he has a bank account where his heart's supposed to be," Loco answered. "We all knew that."

He sat down, and reached out a hand to me. I came over and slid my arms around his neck, gently, and he looked up to me with a trace of a smile.

"Sorry for the really bad welcome," he said.

I grinned at him. "Keeps things exciting, anyway."

I suddenly thought back to the desire that had been running through me just before we walked into the apartment. With the danger past, it made a return. Loco's smile widened slightly. It was pretty obvious he could tell from my expression.

Axel glanced from him to me, and then stood.

"I'd better get to work. Hopefully they haven't fired me already."

Loco nodded at him, and then grabbed his hand for a second.

"I'll walk you to the end of the street, in case that shit-bag is hanging around. Keep your phone on you after that, ok? And I'll pick you up later."

Axel shrugged. "He doesn't know where I work now."

"I think he'd have ways of finding out," Loco replied, firmly. "I'm driving you."

Loco kissed me briefly as he stood.

"I'll be back in a few minutes. Make yourself comfortable."

And then he ran a hand so lightly down my arm that it made me shudder.

"Don't be long," I muttered, and I heard him laugh gently on the way out.

19

IF AT FIRST…

With the Veste boys gone, I spent a while wandering around the small apartment, enjoying things just because they were Loco's. I looked through a stack of CDs in the living-room, both new and old, and liked the fact that he still bought them. All my music is downloads these days, and I often think what a shame it is that I have none of the boxes and album-artwork I used to enjoy.

In the hall, I was reminded of the takeout by the really hunger-inducing smells, and went to find somewhere to keep it all warm. The kitchen had a tiny oven in one corner, so I shoved the food in there and switched it to a low heat. It was pretty big of me not to start eating without him, I thought.

It was difficult to stop thinking about a slightly confused combination of a plateful of food and Loco's chest. A distraction was needed.

I had the perfect one within an instant of sitting at the kitchen table. It was the perfect time to practise controlling the matchmaking. I'd seen Axel again, and had gotten to like him a little bit more.

"OK," I said to myself out loud. "So you need to feel it

happening, and then stop it. Without stopping yourself from liking the guy."

I knew exactly how to make it start happening. I had to really, really want for him to be happy. I thought about Axel's white face when we'd walked in, and how awful Rhett was. I thought about how he'd been an easily-led kid, and they'd taken advantage of him. I thought about his enthusiasm, his beauty, and his sensitivity. And then I thought about how much happier he'd be if he had someone else.

It was frightening how quickly I started to feel it. It was a lot quicker and stronger than it had been in that cafe, which was the only time in the past few years I'd done it on purpose. Usually I spent all my time not thinking about how great people were.

I couldn't see Axel, but I might as well have been able to. I was totally aware of where he was, some half-a-mile distant and walking. The other half of the weird magnetism was further away, across the city, but drawing closer all the time.

"Shit," I said, feeling it growing out of my control. "Stop it. You can do it. Stop it. *Stop it.*"

But it didn't stop. It just kept building, and I knew it was going to keep on going until the two of them met.

"Come on," I said, thinking momentarily of Loco and how much I wanted to make this work.

It only intensified further. I knew it was getting close to the point of being irreversible, and there was only one thing I could do to stop it.

I squeezed my eyes closed, tightly, and remembered Axel's immaturity; his protests about having told Rhett he wouldn't carry drugs for him. I remembered that what he'd carried had had the potential to harm a lot of people. I remembered that he was weak, and that his weakness hurt Loco. He'd had to change his college just for his brother, and his brother was still making his life hard.

The feeling of magnetism began to fade. I held onto the irritation, and in my mind put a sort-of halo of mild annoyance around Axel and everything about him. Pulse by pulse, it dwindled, until I lost any awareness of Loco's brother or the person I'd nearly matched him up with.

I slumped onto the table, feeling exhausted and dejected. My arms and legs were shaking, and I knew part of it was fear for the future. I couldn't control it any more than I could control how I felt about Loco, and I knew how much it was going to tear me apart losing him.

I was still there when Loco let himself back in a little while later. He seemed buoyed-up, and excited, and it made me feel worse. I was going to have to tell him the truth.

"You tried making Axel fall in love with someone, didn't you?" he asked, his eyes alive with enthusiasm. "I could feel it. It's... it's the weirdest thing. I could feel him, and someone else being drawn to him. And he kind-of zoned out, but when I asked if he could feel anything weird, he looked at me like I was crazy." He laughed, and I tried to smile back at him. "And then you stopped it, didn't you? It started to fade. And then it was just gone. You managed to control it."

I shook my head at him, and folded my arms across my chest to try and stop the shaking. "I didn't. I just - I had to tell myself I didn't like him. Which is the only way I've ever stopped it. And I can't do that when I get close to someone. Eventually, I have to stop lying to myself."

I saw the slight disappointment in his expression, but it was quickly replaced with nothing more than concern.

"Hey," he said, coming towards me and kneeling next to me so he could put his arms around me. "Don't be sad. It's the first time you've tried it this way. Give yourself a break and try again later. There's no rush."

I loved the feeling of his arms around me, but I could feel the danger in liking it too much. The sensation of that magnetic draw was too close, and I was already tired from trying to control it.

"Yes there is," I said, and then I grabbed him by the hair and pulled his head around until I could kiss him, fiercely.

Loco was obviously startled, but then he responded, shifting so that I could move my legs and get them around him. I was angry with him, and I hung onto it. I knew I had to.

I gave him a shove, and he toppled backwards onto one arm, with a slight laugh. He pulled at my arm and I lost my balance and crashed down on top of him. My knee hit the floor painfully, and I drew back sharply. I grabbed his hair again.

"Don't - fucking - hurt me," I said, and then locked my mouth on his again.

IT WAS FEROCIOUS, that love-making. Fierce, and physical - the kind that leaves you with bruises and scrapes you don't remember getting. Loco responded to my anger with a fierceness of his own, but where mine was directed at controlling and almost hurting, his was directed at giving in to me. He let me tear at his shirt and his pants, and threw his head back and leaned on his shoulders as I rode him hard and then joined my mouth with his, or bit his ear or his neck.

It was crazy and rage-filled and utterly fantastic. It left us both panting, and slick with sweat. We lay on the floor there, briefly, before Loco wound his arms around me and asked if I'd like to move to the bed.

"OK," I said, the anger abating now. "But only if we can take the food with us."

For the record, it's impossible to eat Thai in bed without getting a lot of it on the sheets. But it's also one of life's best things to do, and I was willing to ignore the satay sauce I ended up lying in as I curled against Loco's chest.

I was tired enough to keep any soppy thoughts away now the anger was gone. I felt that same calm I'd had after we first made love, and I was quite happy just to lie there while he stroked my hair.

"It's going to be ok, you know," he said.

"Is it?"

"Yeah," he said. "I've decided."

I smiled at him. "Who put you in charge?"

He laughed. "I figured it was my turn."

I don't remember falling asleep there, but I remember never, ever wanting to move again.

20

FLIGHT RISK

I mentioned already how rare it is for me to stay until morning. Even the few times a relationship lasted longer than a month, I would usually wake out with my heart pounding in the night, certain I was about to make it happen all over again. And then I'd dress, and I'd leave, and have to pretend it was all part of the cool-and-distant Cally.

So waking up slowly, with daylight in my eyes and Loco slumped unconscious half over me, was both disorientating and delicious.

I twisted a little so I could look at him, asleep and unaware and slack-jawed, with just a little bit of dried drool on his chin. He was still perfect. It made me ache.

And then I sat up, quickly and with my heart pounding, as I felt a flutter of that magnetic power.

"Enough," I whispered to myself, and picked up my phone. I knew I needed a distraction before that thinking went any further. I sort-of hate the constant connectivity of cell-phones with email, but there's no denying that they're good for taking your mind off things. Within five seconds of loading up my web browser, I can have forgotten what I was logging on for, and only surface an hour later.

I usually start with email. I like to see my inbox show a batch of new messages, which I know will mostly be from crappy mailing lists I signed up to without knowing, or in order to enter some prize draw I've forgotten about. Every few months I try and do a purge of unsubscribing but it never seems to make the problem go away.

Today, there were twelve new messages, and the first one I locked onto was from my Mom, who was asking for the third time what I wanted for Christmas. I guessed I'd better reply today. She'd gotten to the stage of using capital letters for emphasis. And were there really only three shopping days left?

I scrolled up, and zipped past three offers from restaurants I hadn't enjoyed that much the first time. I almost didn't stop on the one from admin@nasacareers.org, but then the words sunk in and I was suddenly a million miles from Loco.

WE ARE PLEASED to offer you an interview on January 3rd…

THEY WANTED TO INTERVIEW ME. NASA wanted to actually talk to me. Despite the thousands of applications and the tiny chance of success, I was down to the final fifty candidates.

I sat staring at it for a good few minutes without moving, and then, more as something to do than because I particularly cared about other messages, I clicked onwards.

"Fuck," I said, and it was loud enough to wake Loco up.

"Is that an order?" he murmured, and squinted at me.

"It's - I've had an email. Look."

I held my cell-phone out to him with a hand that shook, and he blinked at it.

"OK. You're going to have to read it out to me. My eyes don't work before eight am."

I wasn't quite sure that I could, but I tried to paraphrase it.

"It's from the Mars mission. They - they want me for the second phase. Even if I don't get into NASA, they want me."

"Sorry, what?" he asked, and sat up, adjusting a couple of pillows so he was no longer horizontal and then tugging at my arm until I sat back next to him. The way his arm went around me felt like the easiest, most natural thing in the world.

"The Mars mission," I said again. "I applied for it. They're going to send two people every two years, to start a colony there. They take applicants from all over the world. I applied six months ago and didn't hear anything so I figured... but I'm first choice for the second phase. So in five years I could be - I could be on Mars."

Loco went very still. I could hear his heart through his chest, and it was thumping as hard as mine was.

"You want to go to Mars?" he said at last. "For real?"

"I always wanted to," I said, not quite answering the question.

"This colony," he went on, slowly. "It's a one-way trip, isn't it? They can't fund bringing anyone back, no matter what. So that would be it. In five years, goodbye earth."

"Yeah, it would."

"Why would anyone want to do that?" he asked, mystified.

"Because it's the most important step in space discovery the human race will have made," I said, immediately.

There was a pause, and then Loco asked, "And why would *you* want to do that?"

It still cut me a little, that way he had of seeing past every wall I threw up.

"Wouldn't it sound perfect to you?" I whispered. "If you were lonely all the time, and knew you'd lose everyone in the end?

The Cupid Touch

They send two at a time, so no matter what happens, there will always be someone who won't fall in love with someone else. There'll always be a friend, or maybe a lover. For years and years. I wouldn't have to spend the rest of my life being torn to pieces every time I made someone fall in love."

I could feel him nodding, and then feel the soft touch of a kiss on my forehead.

"It would," he said. "If I were twenty-something and I'd lost all those people. But what about the Cally of now? Who's found someone, too? Someone who's not planning on going anywhere? And what if that Cally learned to control it? What would you want to do then?"

I was silent for a long time. It wasn't because it was a difficult question to answer, but because I still couldn't imagine ever being in control of what I did.

"I don't know," I said, with a shrug and a small smile. "I guess that Cally might want to stay."

"Might, huh?" he asked, sliding his hand up the inside of my thigh. "You still want some convincing?"

He kissed me, and I folded my arms round him and moved my legs apart to let his hand climb further. I was already hot and wet with the feel of him when I remembered that other email. I drew back, and gave him a grin.

"There are other options for space, I guess," I said. "Guess who got an interview for NASA?"

He studied my face, and then smiled broadly.

"You know, if you keep kicking this much ass, I might end up liking you for keeps."

"I'll try to avoid it," I said, my hand going to find his ass. I couldn't get enough of how toned it was.

"So," he said, as his fingers slid upwards over my clitoris and made every muscle in my abdomen squeeze with pleasure. "What are we going to do today?"

"Work?" I asked.

"Try harder," he said, bending his head to suck gently on my right nipple.

"Well, we went star-gazing," I said, trying to concentrate and increasingly failing. "So maybe... something you like to do..."

"I'll be kind-of tired," he said, breaking off for a moment and murmuring it. "I have practice this afternoon."

"You think that's going to be the most tiring thing you do today?" I asked him, and moved my hand around to the base of his once-more hard cock.

"Willing to learn differently," he answered.

I WENT to watch him at practice once I'd done a good seven hours in the computer-lab. My eyes were tired and my brain melted and I'd stopped doing anything that resembled careful work. The strange thing was that I was able to concentrate on the work. Thoughts of Loco didn't interrupt in the way I'd expected. I kept just imagining acing the project and getting to tell Loco. If he were half as pleased as he'd been about the NASA thing, it was still an awesome motivation.

I have to admit to being as vain as ever when I got ready to see him. I'd brought a bag full of hot, warm little pants and tops outfits, all of them designed to look effortlessly attractive. They were also about as far from the trophy girlfriend look as I could manage, which was another sort of vanity I guess.

It still felt like a betrayal of my feminist principles walking up to take a seat on the stands. I could see a cluster of other players' girlfriends further down the field and most of them were freezing their asses off in short skirts. Were we all just going to admire the big strong men?

I sat awkwardly on the front row a good twenty yards from them, and spent a while trying to work out which one was Loco as they practised sprints and kicks, and then separated for a game. And then I saw one of them moving in a way I knew, jogging easily down from the far end of the pitch to get to his team-mates, and I couldn't help smiling. Even from this distance, and in all that padding, he looked hot.

He saw me at the same time. He lifted his visor and pulled out his mouth-guard, then kept on that loping jog until he was at the stands in front of me.

"Whatcha doing, Taylor?" he asked, grinning.

"Watching your ass do its thing," I answered. "The usual."

I couldn't help smiling at him, and leaning down a little closer. He gave me a kiss straight on the mouth, before putting the guard back in and running backwards for a minute.

"Maybe you should wear that later," I called. "You look hot."

"You fucking bet," was what I think he shouted back, before he joined the game.

To my total shame, I was not only grinning like an idiot, but also feeling utterly smug about the girlfriends and admirers all turning around to look at me.

I'VE NEVER APPRECIATED football much. I like to claim it's because it's boring, and because there's no fun when everyone where's that much shielding, but actually it's the opposite. I flinch every time someone takes a hit or runs into someone, in a way I probably wouldn't if it was me doing it. It's one thing to go and get into what basically amounts to a large-scale public fight over a ball, and another one to watch helplessly as other people take a bruising. (I told you I have that heart in there somewhere, despite my best efforts).

Of course, it was worse when I was watching Loco. I cringed to watch him end up underneath a pile of two-hundred pound guys, and felt a flood of relief every time he clambered back up and ran. But after a little while I began to notice that he was taking hits a lot less often than most of them, and that he was really, really fast. I started appreciating the power in those legs as well as their aesthetic side, and to be genuinely awed at how he seemed to be able to predict the game. Wherever the play went, there would be Loco, at the ready and totally unstoppable once he got going.

It became difficult not to turn into a cheerleader as the practise progressed. I was half off my seat as he charged up the field, and I gave out an involuntary "woop!" when he was the one to score a touch-down against his team-mates.

I also started to notice that Loco's tactics were less egotistical football-star and more leader of a pack he cared about. He'd only been here a couple of weeks, and yet he talked to them all, slung an arm around them, and protected them. He talked to the coach a lot, too, a pepper-haired, bulky man in his forties who seemed to laugh a lot more than I'd have expected.

In fact, only one of the players seemed to have a problem with Loco. He was playing against him, and he shadowed him, taking every opportunity to take him down, block him, or (I started to think) just kick or punch him. It didn't seem to worry him too much, and I felt no rush of anger or vengeance. Loco just seemed able to shrug off bad-feeling and move on.

By the end of the game, I had started to see how easy it would be to get hooked on all this. It was a rush watching one of them break out of the pack and sprint down the field, and it was even better when it was Loco.

The group clustered around their coach, presumably for a team-talk on how it had gone. The chat went on for ten minutes longer than I'd have thought, while I got a little colder in the growing darkness. I wondered if I ought to leave and text Loco to meet me, but after he'd exchanged a few remarks with some of them, he jogged back over to me, taking his helmet off his sweat-plastered hair and grinning at me.

"Glad you stuck around."

"And I'm glad you still have all your teeth," I said, leaning to kiss him over the rail. "Good practise?"

"Yeah," he said, "in spite of Durrant gunning for me."

He looked over at that one player who had dogged him, still not particularly angry as far as I could make out.

"What's his problem?" I asked.

"Ah, we had a few words at the start of the game," he said, with a shrug. And I could immediately tell that those words had been about me by the way he said it.

"What?"

"Ah, he just - He asked me if 'the Ice Queen' was a good lay. He's an asshole. Don't worry about him."

I felt pretty Ice Queen-ish just then. My stomach went cold and a little bit despairing. I didn't even know the guy, and he still had a cruel name for me.

"What'd you say?" I asked Loco, trying to sound like it didn't matter.

"I said no, of course not," Loco said immediately, sounding a little surprised. "I told him you were a totally amazing person in every way, and if he wanted some lessons in how to talk about women then he knew where to find me. I guess he took me up on it."

I couldn't help laughing, though it was a really emotional kind of a laugh.

"Did I tell you that you're perfect?" I asked him.

"You did," he said, pulling me half over the rail to rest his head against mine. "But I didn't believe you."

I hugged him tightly, and then let him go.

"You'd better go shower, sweat-boy."

"I'm on it," he said, backing away. "Give me half an hour. And go and sit in the sports-cafe. You'll freeze out here." He turned away, and then back again. "I have casual clothes or less-casual clothes. Which ones do you want me in?"

"You think I want you in clothes…?" I called.

He laughed and shouted out, "I guess that's casual, then."

I tried not to think too hard about just how crazy I was about him as he disappeared into the locker-rooms.

21

DEEPEST RED

It hadn't been hard to decide where to take Loco for the evening. There was a place I'd been meaning to go back to ever since I'd stopped off there in the middle of a bike loop and not wanted to leave.

It was an old hunting-lodge at the edge of Breakheart Reservation, the collection of lakes and woods out towards Salem. It had become an eaterie at some point, and my guess was that the decor had changed a lot. It looked how you felt a hunting-lodge *should* look - all dark colours, fireplaces, bare stone and wood. It had tapestries on the walls and occasional trophies (though not enough of them for it to get uncomfortable for the squeamish. I mean, who wants to eat something with a stuffed example of the animal looking down at you off the wall?). You also ate your food sitting in high-backed, red leather easy chairs that were comfy enough to live in.

"Are we going to kill and eat a bear?" Loco asked me as we followed his Sat Nav to the postcode I'd punched in. A dose of rain had turned into hail-stones, and it was difficult to see anything but trees. "If so, I volunteer to guard the car."

"You can stay in the car if you like," I told him, "while I eat all the food and fall asleep in a corner."

"While you snore?"

"Possibly."

"I'd better come in," he said, nodding. "You're pretty hot when you snore."

"I'm not rising to that," I said, scratching my nails gently along his arm.

Loco shivered in response. "You are the most distracting passenger I know."

"Distracting? I haven't even *started* on distracting."

The lights of the Old Hunter loomed out of the hailstorm and Loco gave me a grin as he drew the car into the lot.

"I just realised I recognise this place."

"You do?" I asked, a little disappointed.

"Yeah. But when I knew it, it was a fishing-shop. My Dad came here a couple times when fishing the lake. It was really depressing, and there were flies all over everything because they had the bait out in tubs. I used to hate coming in with him."

"Don't tell me that!" I protested.

He laughed. "Am I ruining the atmosphere for you? Is Miss Taylor being sentimental?"

He took off his seat-belt to give me a patronising kiss, both hands on my face, so I nipped him lightly on the lower lip.

"So spiky," he said, with a sigh.

"Weird how much you seem to like it," I said, and climbed out of the car. I kept my face well down against the storm and ran for the door, Loco hustling in after me and finishing up standing behind me with his arms around me. I was in no hurry to move as we waited for someone to come and seat us. I leaned back against him and felt that warm contentment that seemed to happen around him.

"See? I'm not always spiky," I said, tilting my head back

towards him. He was in the middle of giving me a really inappropriately sexy kiss when one of the waitresses rocked up and tried to pretend it wasn't awkward.

I waited for Loco to look around the place, which he finally did after we'd ordered.

"Is it... non-good being reminded of your Dad?"

He glanced back at me, quickly. "No, it - actually, it doesn't remind me much. It's so different. And it's a really nice place now. My Dad would never have come here. He was a fast-food and liquor kind of guy."

"Does Axel know?" I asked. "About you, and... and what happened."

"Ah, no, he doesn't." He suddenly looked a little embarrassed. "I mean, it's not an easy one to confess as you'll know. And aside from the likelihood he'd think I was crazy, I didn't want - he's my kid brother. I'm supposed to protect everyone. I didn't like the idea of him looking at me like I was a killer. You know?"

He looked forlorn again, less the dangerous, muscular football star who could rain down vengeance and more the kid who'd been desperate to keep his Mom safe.

"Yeah," I said. "I know."

I drank down the little squeeze of my heart for him with the pale craft beer we'd been served with, and then I started talking about his football until I could see the tension leave him. Little by little, throughout eating, we crept closer and closer to each other, until it was easier to vacate my chair and go and squeeze onto the side of Loco's with him. There was nobody within sight, and I could feel the familiar heat rising in me as he wound his fingers in my hair.

"You know, they have rooms upstairs," I murmured. "We could always stay..."

He laughed. "How much would that cost?"

"Not much," I said. "And you know, there's no point making your Mom fall for a ridiculously rich man if you don't get to abuse it a little."

"And you think it's still ok?" he asked, quietly. "You're not worried about making anything happen?"

I stopped and thought about it, trying to keep it purely theoretical and not allow any access to that magnetic draw that would steal him away forever. "I am," I said. "But it's hard worrying about it all the time. I'd like - I guess I should be practising the control thing."

"Can you do it now?" he asked. "While I watch?"

He was still twining his fingers through the hair at the back of my neck, and the last thing I wanted right then was to control myself and think about Axel's perfect match.

"Is this the entertainment for the evening?" I asked.

"Jeez, I hope not," he said, and kissed the side of my neck so softly that I shuddered.

"Ahhh, I can't do it when you're doing that." With a sigh, I stood up, and went to sit back in my own chair.

"Well that's less fun," he said.

"Do you want me to practise or not?" I asked, glaring at him.

"Well, if it's a choice between you practising and having to fall in love with some other woman I don't actually know," he said, "I guess I'll sit here for a few minutes. But only for a few."

I tried not to smile. "You'll have to be quiet."

"I always am."

I took a few deep breaths, pushing away thoughts of a private room upstairs and instead thinking about Axel in a very different sort of way. I thought about how scared he must have been when Rhett turned up and threatened him, and how lost he was. I thought about the frightened boy thinking his Dad might kill his Mom, and how much better it would be if he had someone.

And there it was, that huge drawing feeling, like a hum in the air. I could sense two points at a great distance across the city, one an unknown and the other unmistakably Axel. I tried to hold onto that feeling of caring about him, and then to push the other point away.

I wasn't even sure it was possible, but maybe I could just keep them apart. I wanted him to be happy, but not with the unknown, possibly untrustworthy person who was being reeled in towards him by my power.

I gave a tiny growl of frustration. That other point was still approaching, and the draw was building. Not quickly, but building all the same.

So maybe you need to stop Axel being magnetic, I thought.

I focused as hard as I could on Axel and, whilst still caring about him, tried to put a barrier around him in my mind.

"I can feel it from here," Loco murmured.

It almost broke my concentration. I grabbed hold of that point in my mind, remembering that it was Axel, and that I wanted to help him but also protect him from what I did.

And then something went strange. My heart started to pound and it was as if that point had become an urgent, flashing light instead of a simple marker.

I jerked upright in my chair, unable to feel anything now except dread.

"There's something wrong," I said, my breath short.

"What do you mean?" Loco reached out to take my hand, at once stroking it, soothing me.

"It's Axel. Something's wrong."

I felt his hand tighten on mine.

"You know where he is?" he asked.

"Yeah, I can - I can feel it. It's weird. He's downtown."

Loco was on his feet and pulling his jacket on, his hand scrabbling in his pocket for his cell-phone.

I stood up too, shaking. I knew I had to hold onto the connection with Axel, because chances were, if he was in danger, he wasn't going to be able to answer a call. But Loco was trying anyway.

I tried to focus while I pulled a fifty out of my pocket and threw it down to cover the food. I knew it was too much, but there was no time for anything else.

Please be ok. Please be ok, I thought, and then added, as I thought about charging in on a drug-dealer's heavies to save him, *And please let us be ok, too.*

22

CLUBBING

I could hear the ringing coming through Loco's cell-phone the whole way to the car. It must have rung ten times by the time we got there, with no sound of interruption. It was an ominous sign, and I could see Loco trying to control his panic as much as I was trying to control mine.

And then, as he pulled his car-key out, the ringing was interrupted, and I could hear Axel's "Luca?" from where I stood.

"Axel? Where are you?"

Loco sounded angry, but I knew it was fear making his voice tight.

I could have cried with relief that Axel was still in a position to take a call, but there wasn't time. Instead I ran around to the passenger side and let myself in with shaking hands.

"Wait, wait," he was saying into the phone as I closed the door. "You're going too..."

There was a burst of hurried talking, and Loco nodded.

"OK. Do it. I'm coming to pick you up in around thirty minutes. I'll call you when I'm outside. Come out with someone, ok?"

He hung up, and started the engine with a roar.

"He's in a night-club," he said, answering the question I hadn't needed to ask. "He was on the road home and a car crawled up alongside. He recognised one of Rhett's guys, and he turned straight into the door of the club. He used to date one of the bar staff, so he's going to get behind the bar where they can't man-handle him out."

I nodded, my heart a painful thump in my throat. I hoped Loco was right, and they couldn't simply threaten Axel's ex to get him out of there. The world of organised, violent crime was not one I'd ever had a particular interest in getting to know.

"What are you going to do?" I asked Loco, holding onto a handle on the door briefly as he took a corner at speed. "I mean - not right now. In the long-term."

"I don't know," he replied, in a low voice. "I'll do everything I can not to make things... bad, but -"

He didn't have to explain any more. I knew that Axel meant more to him than the life of a drug-dealing ex-boyfriend and his stooges. And I didn't expect him to have a lot of sympathy for his boss, either.

"It's going to be hard controlling it if they're threatening him," he added.

I slid my hand around his elbow and rubbed his skin with my thumb. "I'll do what I can to help."

He turned a very serious gaze on me for a moment. "Don't come inside. I know you'll want to be there, and won't appreciate me being over-protective. But I'm probably about to really piss these guys off, and I'd prefer it if they didn't have someone else to aim at."

It's pretty crappy to admit it, but a large part of me was relieved. I didn't want to walk in there. But at the same time, I didn't want him walking in there, either.

"If you're sure," I said, and then added, "but I'm going to be right outside with the car, whatever you say. You're going to need a fast exit strategy."

He grinned, slightly. "Hidden depths," he said.

"What, as a criminal mastermind?" I asked.

"No, I just didn't know you could drive..."

I shoved him gently, trying to hold on to the humour while that urgent note of alarm pulsed in my mind.

Axel called again once we were on the edge of the city, telling Loco to come to the back of the club.

"That's good," Loco said, once he'd hung up. "There's a staff entrance to an alley where they get rid of the trash. You can't get in that way, only out. Which means you can drop me close by and drive round to the alley-way. We'll come straight to you, and it keeps you out of sight."

He pulled into a side-road a few blocks from the nightclub, and climbed out of the driver's seat so I could climb in.

"I'll walk from here," he said, catching me briefly and kissing me before I could get in. "You know where you're going?"

"I've got it," I said, trying to smile at him. "Be careful, Loco."

He kissed me again, with a smile, and then headed to the busy main street while I negotiated the car around the corner and onto the narrow alley that ran around the back of the shops and clubs on the street.

I had a sudden worry that I didn't really know where I was going. It was the back door of Belusci's, and I knew basically where that was, but there were no signs on this side. It was all just metal doors and dumpsters.

Five blocks down, though, I passed a door with a small sign on that had the MacDonald's logo on, and I knew that was close to Belusci's. I drew the car in close to the wall opposite a steel door and switched off the engine.

The reality of waiting for the brothers to emerge hit me the moment I was on my own in the car. I had no idea what was going on in there, and I had no way of telling whether silence from Loco meant all was going well or that all was going wrong. All I could feel from my awareness of Axel not far away was that the threat was still there.

As time passed (twelve incredibly slow minutes by my obstinately silent cell-phone screen) I began to feel really afraid. Axel might be ok, if still in danger, but what if Loco had run into some of the ones sent to get his brother? Rhett knew who he was. I had no way of knowing whether he'd made it inside.

My palm started to sweat where I was holding the phone. I was itching to call him, just to hear him tell me that he was ok.

Fifteen minutes.

How could it take fifteen minutes? He only needed to walk two blocks, grab Axel and leave the club.

I needed to drown out that internal voice, and so I started talking to myself instead, out loud.

"Axel was probably busy talking to his ex. Or maybe they had to hide while someone went past. They'll be fine."

Seventeen excruciating minutes, that felt like a life-time.

"OK, so this is useful. You have now ruled out a career as a get-away driver. It sucks."

I was looking so hard at the smooth, slightly dented metal door that I started to think I might melt through it with my eyes.

"That would be a so much more useful super-power," I muttered to myself.

It had hit 10:48 on my phone, a full twenty minutes after I'd left Loco, when my gaze was drawn away temporarily by movement in the alley-way. I would have ignored the two men in leather coats and black pants who were walking oh-so-casually past if one of them hadn't nodded towards me, and then stopped to say something to his companion in what was clearly a low voice.

Oh, shit.

I glanced away, as if I were just waiting and bored. I lifted my phone to my face, not able to remember how I acted when I was being casual.

My mouth had turned into some kind of desert, and by the time I glanced past the screen again, the two of them had started walking again. My vague hope that they actually weren't anything to do with us died pretty quickly when they stopped at the metal door to the club and one of them drew out something metal and slid it into the frame.

The other one glanced at me again, and I looked back at my cell-phone and gave a theatrical sigh.

I'm a bored girlfriend, I thought, as I brought up Loco's number on the phone as well as I could with sweaty, half-numb fingers. I don't care about you and your obvious criminal intentions.

The moment the guy looked away, I pressed the call button, praying that Loco would hear or feel his phone even with the noise and the press of the club.

Nothing happened, and I slumped back in my seat, half trying to hide the phone and half trying to pretend that I was just pissed off at being made to wait for someone.

Come on, come on...

And then Loco's voice was in my ear, surprisingly clear and free of noise.

"Are you-"

"There are two men forcing open the back door," I said, cutting across him. "They'll be in in about ten seconds."

"Are they armed?"

He sounded pretty cool, all things considered.

"I don't think so, I haven't..."

And then I made the mistake of looking up to check, at the moment the guy looked over again.

I felt cold as our eyes met. Totally cold. I was frozen there, and I knew my face was telling him everything.

Very slowly, his eyes narrowed, and his hand reached towards his jacket pocket. I didn't get how he could move. I couldn't seem to do anything except sit there, the cold draining away and a terrible heat taking its place.

Which was the only warning I had before the metal door blasted open as if something had exploded behind it. The guy who'd been trying to force it went down like a dead weight, and the other one was sent staggering after the edge of it clipped his arm.

Like an unstoppable force, Loco was suddenly there, and on him, grabbing him by the throat and hurling him back into the door as it bounced off the wall. The guys head snapped forwards as it met the metal, and I flinched, unable to help a pang of sympathy.

Loco didn't seem to feel the same. He swung him round and brought a knee up into his groin. I saw something fall from the guy's hand, and realised that he had been armed after all. It was a small, black, but unmistakably deadly gun that clattered to the ground.

As Loco swung, I saw the apparently unconscious guy on the ground move. I had my mouth open to shout in warning, but I wasn't even nearly in time.

The sound of a gun going off in close proximity was utterly unreal. It wasn't loud enough, and yet it rang in my ears for what seemed like hours afterwards.

Loco didn't seem surprised. Even after the bullet had found its home, he was calm as he kicked the gun out of the guy's hand and then stamped on the exposed fingers.

He wasn't quite in time to catch the guy he'd kneed in the groin. He sagged, and his knees hit the tarmac. He pressed his hands to his stomach and looked up at Loco with an expression of mild surprise.

The bullet hit him, I thought. Loco's ok. He's ok.

I pretty much fell out of the car as I hurried out. I couldn't seem to make my legs and arms work, and when Axel emerged from the club at the same time I could see my shock mirrored on his face.

The feeling of heat was suddenly gone, and I was shaking with cold as well as the after-effects of fear.

Loco looked up at me, his eyes large but his face calm. He gave me a strange half-smile, that somehow reminded me of someone crying.

"We need an ambulance," he said, briefly, and then surprisingly gently laid one of the two guys who'd tried to shoot him onto his back and pressed his hands over the wound in his stomach.

23

NERVE ENDINGS

"It's on its way."

I'd called for the ambulance, weirdly calm about it, and then bent down to try and help Loco with the wounded hood.

I'd been so terrified for Luca that I hadn't noticed what I should have done. The magnetic awareness of Axel had shifted focus. It was Loco I could sense now: Loco and another distant point that was drawing nearer. In my flood of relief that he was ok, I was close to losing control of it.

Don't love him. Don't love him. Come on, Cally!

It was terrifying. I could feel myself growing sweaty with fear. It was like the prelude to throwing up.

But then I caught Luca's gaze, and it was cold and distant and not at all part of the haze of love.

"Thank you for doing that," Loco said, as if I were some kind of a stranger. "Sorry you walked in on it. Are you ok with blood?"

"I'm... fine," I said, feeling actually a little bit sick still and seriously confused. Had something snapped in him? Or was this what he was really, truly like when he got angry? Cold and distant and... inhuman.

It was strange going pretty quickly from fear of Luca Veste dying to fear of Luca Veste himself. Whatever had happened, it did the swiftest job I could remember of nuking the magnetic feeling. It faded out as if it had never existed. But I couldn't feel good about it.

"Are you all right?" I asked him. "I..."

"My brother and I were just leaving," he cut in. "I think we must have walked in on some kind of a hit."

He glanced up at me, significantly, and a sort of a light dawned. He was trying to pretend he didn't know me, because only one of the guys was unconscious.

I gave him a slow nod, and then looked instinctively at the guy with the gunshot wound. He looked bad. His skin was sort-of greyish, and he there was sweat standing out on it, but he was shivering.

"Are you ok?" I asked him.

"I just - I don't feel good."

Which was pretty natural, given he'd been shot in the stomach, but he didn't seem to be losing all that much blood.

"I think he's in shock," I said, remembering being hit by it myself the time I broke my ankle. "I've got a can of soda in my bag."

I went to get it, trying to act like it was my car I was going to and not Loco's, and of course, messing up opening the door. But I wasn't so sure the injured guy was in any state to notice.

I grabbed the soda and crouched back next to him. He flinched when I pulled the ring, but let me tilt some into his mouth.

"You need some sugar," I said, hoping that I wasn't doing the wrong thing feeding him liquid when he had abdominal injuries. But shock can kill more quickly than blood loss, and I wasn't going to let Loco end up being charged for murder. Even if he hadn't actually touched the gun.

Axel came to sit next to me, almost as grey as the injured guy.

"Shit," he said, quietly, as he looked at the blood that was gradually welling between Luca's fingers.

I could feel all of us flinch when the first sound of a siren made it to us. It was an intermingled wail that resolved itself into two squad cars and an ambulance. They had to go pretty slowly to fit down the alley, and then the squad cars had to park up behind and squeeze past the ambulance. It was all in all almost funny.

The ambulance didn't stay long. Two paramedics loaded up both the hoods and screamed (kind-of-slowly) off. Which was when the questions started from the three cops who'd turned up.

I could see them watching Loco steadily while he talked, and their questions were a little bit skeptical.

"Why were you exiting the back of the nightclub?... Can I see your knuckles? Are those bruises?"

But once they'd asked us all the same questions and come up with the same answers - that I was waiting while Luca picked up his brother, that I was Luca's girlfriend, that Axel knew some of the staff there - they seemed to become less suspicious, and more accepting. It was just unfortunate that Luca had opened the door at the wrong time and interrupted some kind of a confrontation. It was a shame one of the guys assumed he was being attacked and went for him.

"If there are any assault charges brought against me, I'll take them," Luca said levelly, at one point. "Though given the guy had just shot someone, I'm hoping that won't be relevant."

They took all our names, and the name of Axel's ex-boyfriend bartender, and then they let us go.

I couldn't stop looking at the blood outside the door

throughout all of it, and I was still staring at it as Luca drove us away.

"You're leaving," Loco said, turning to talk over his shoulder to Axel. "On the first train I can put you on."

"What about work?" his brother asked.

"What about your life?" Luca snapped back. "You can't be in this city while they're looking for you."

"But it's not going to go away," Axel argued. "What's the point in running?"

"It will," Loco said quietly.

It made my flesh crawl, hearing him say it.

He met my gaze when I looked over at him, and I know what I was thinking was obvious: that he'd promised not to bring revenge down on them if he could avoid it.

"You have some magical method?" Axel asked, sounding a little bit like he was twelve.

"The cops are involved now," Luca said. "I'm going to give them a lot more information on Rhett. I think they'll be interested in him and his boss."

Axel gave a sigh. "It could take months to do it that way. And I'm pretty sure the cops already know about them. It's proving it that's the problem."

"I'll make it happen," Luca said, and reached out to take my hand. I squeezed it, harder than I had to, trying to somehow communicate that he had to try it the right way. I saw a small smile appear on his face. He knew what I was saying.

"Where am I going to go?" Axel seemed to have accepted his brother's decision, even if he was being a little sullen about it. I guessed that he was pretty scared underneath the irritation at having his life interrupted.

"Uncle Aaron's."

"Seriously?" Axel asked, leaning forward. "It's miles from anything."

"Yup," Loco said. "And nobody's going to know you're there."

"They know who you are now, you know, bro," Axel said, suddenly serious. "You need to be careful too."

"I'm on it," he said, sounding serenely unworried. "You worry about yourself, little brother. And until you are on that train, you are not leaving my sight. Got it?"

Axel huffed, and I laughed, because it was about time someone did.

"Bossy big brother, much?" I asked.

Luca glanced at me, and smiled slightly. "Bossy boyfriend too. Be grateful none of them knows who you are, or I'd be walking you everywhere."

I grinned at him, and only then remembered the guy looking at me as I spoke to Luca on the phone, and the recognition on his face. I could feel the blood draining out of my face, but by that point, Luca had already turned to look back at the road.

We didn't get our night in a hunting-lodge hotel. We didn't get total privacy. We got to sleep in a room that shared a wall with Axel's, and listen to the quiet buzzing of the bass through his speakers. But after I'd been through the terror of losing Luca in two ways today, there was no way I was going to be self-controlled.

I could sense the same urgent desire in Luca the moment the door closed, and in absolute silence we undressed each other and pressed mouths, bodies, legs together in a slow and achingly wonderful love-making. I bit Luca's shoulder hard enough to leave marks to keep from making any sound, and when I put the palm of my hand up to his mouth as he got a little noisy, he grabbed it between his teeth. Just then, I loved the pain. It made me a little bit angry, and it was so much better than being scared that I embraced it as I gave in to him all over again.

24

THE CLOSING NET

I didn't sleep all that well. Lying wound up in Luca's arms didn't stop my mind starting to drip-feed me images of that guy outside the club. It would start with a squeeze of disbelieving worry that Loco could have been responsible for killing him, and a hope that he had survived. And then it would bounce from there to the vivid memory of him looking at me through the car window, while I met his eyes and knew for certain that he'd caught me out. And then I'd think about telling Luca, which would bring out a more insidious fear: that he would insist I had to go away, and that in missing him from a distance I'd kick off that magnetic process and lose him forever. The fear of it would lead to hoping that maybe the guy with the gun wouldn't survive, and then I'd feel terrible for thinking it, which would lead me right back to the beginning.

Even when I did sleep, it was fitful and interrupted. At six I crashed out of a weird dream where Axel had been told to kill me by Rhett and decided he'd better do it. I was too wired with the adrenaline of seeing Loco's brother point a gun at me to sleep again, so I gave up and extricated myself from under one of Luca's arms. He was snoring very quietly, his mouth all slack and totally not-sexy. It was hard not to find it adorable, which was another reason for making a sharp exit.

I pulled my clothes on, a little bit smug about quite how much they'd ended up scattered around the room, and brushed my teeth (with Luca's tooth-brush, which he'd told me to use the night before - cue worry about having bad breath without realising it. I hate being an idiot about that kind of thing). After that I retrieved my phone and started browsing the morning news while the coffee-machine heated up, leaning against the counter and giving my calves a stretch at the same time.

There was, as always, a lot that was wrong with the world. CNN's website was leading with a shooting, and I couldn't even bring myself to read about Syria after the first two paragraphs mentioned two thousand civilian casualties this week.

I was looking for something more cheerful to read when I caught sight of a starry image on the side-bar that I knew well.

It made me feel weird to read the headline: "Astronomers Confirm Nearby System Going Nova."

I clicked through to a too-brief article about Eta Carinae, and wasn't surprised to see that one Dr. Brandon Larsen was quoted in it.

"IT'S A VERY EXCITING OCCURRENCE," Dr. Larsen comments. "This is by far the closest supernova we will have witnessed, with the potential effects on the Earth's atmosphere itself, although they are unlikely to be noticeable to ordinary people. It's not an apocalypse scenario."

I could imagine how smug he'd sounded when he'd said it. It was quite hard not feeling like I hated Axel's boyfriend just then, which was not even slightly rational.

It's not you and Luca, I tried telling myself. But as I looked at pictures of those two stars, one blazing brightly and close to self-destruction, I couldn't help seeing the two of us torn apart. It felt like the floor I was standing on was falling.

I jumped when I felt a pair of hands slide around my shoulders. Luca was sleepy and warm, and it did a lot to cut through the chill on my skin.

"It's too cold to be up," he muttered into my ear.

"Look at this," I said, and held the phone up where he could see it.

"Didn't I tell you I don't do reading before ten am?" he asked, but he took the phone, coming to stand next to me with his arm around my shoulders.

"Oh, neat," he said. "You feeling all excited about it, astro-geek?"

He looked at me, sidelong, and I could tell he remembered what I'd said at the observatory.

"I don't know. I still think it's kind-of sad," I answered. I leaned into him as closely as I could, borrowing his warmth through his slacks and nicely tight t-shirt.

He kissed the top of my head. "Just as long as you're only worrying about those poor little stars, and not assuming we're doomed. I'm not keen on you trying to run away again."

"I don't think we're doomed," I said, automatically, and there was a buzz in his chest as he laughed.

"You're such a liar."

"OK," I said, half-smiling. "I feel like it's about fifty-fifty right now. But I'm not going to run away. I promise. You worry about your brother and the crazy criminals. We're just fine."

"Good," he said. "Though you know what'd make us even better? Being in a nice, warm, comfortable bed..."

I tipped my head back and he gave me a slow, warm, sexy kiss.

"I'm not going to argue with that."

I got Luca to drop me at on campus before he took Axel for

his train. He'd called up their Uncle and arranged it all. Axel would be collected from Charlotte late in the evening, after a pretty horrific-sounding journey. But anything is better than being hunted down and killed, and Axel didn't complain about it all that much on the way there. He was largely too busy leaning forward to tell me what Brandon had messaged him about the upcoming supernova.

"He sounded pretty busy," he told me, "but hopefully he'll be able to patch me into some of the real-time radar results later on. It should all happen over the next twenty-four hours. I mean, obviously it's already happened. But for us."

By the time I climbed out of the car I was almost beginning to feel positive about astronomical events. Axel's enthusiasm was difficult to resist.

"I'll come find you after practice," Luca told me, through the open passenger-door.

I gave him a smile, which was almost comfortable and optimistic, and then went to shut myself in the computer lab for seven hours and try not to think about either of the Veste boys too much.

It turned out I did a pretty ok job of that. I was still in the actual coding part of the project, rather than in the dreaded write-up, and it's weirdly possible to zone everything out when you're trying to do something new and get it right. In my case, the project was a modelling one. I wanted to be able to code a quicker way of modelling probable planet characteristics based on the glimpse we get when that planet passes between us and its sun.

It was more complex than the examples we'd been given, and presented a challenge, but I knew that was the only way to make me want to do it. It had to be something I loved, or the project would have been something to put off until after Christmas and then swear over.

I was lost somewhere in a world of C++ when the buzz of my phone woke me up. I looked at it in confusion, realising that it was already four pm and that Loco was texting to say he was free. I hadn't remembered to have any lunch.

Texting him back, I saw the date on my phone and realised with another jolt that I only had two days left before I was heading home for the vacation. All my worries about being sent away from Luca, and I'd forgotten that I was about to leave anyway. It's weird how easy it is to bury your head in the sand.

I finished up saving my work - which I thought might just be two thirds of the project already done - and logged off. I realised then quite how out-of-it I'd been. The three other students in the lab had all left, and even the reception staff had headed off home. I guess there's not much point manning a desk for one person.

I went to meet Loco in the growing gloom of the empty courtyard. I was gradually losing the excitement that went with the coding project, and the darkness and the grey clouds overhead added to the realisation that I would have to say goodbye to Luca for a couple of weeks. I felt suddenly down, which is not something I've ever associated with the few days before Christmas.

I climbed onto a picnic table and pulled my feet up onto the bench as I waited for him. The gloom seemed to be settling in, so I did my part ɪ feeling-crappy self-care and told myself I'd feel better once I'd had something to eat, and that everything was fine. Then I tried it out loud.

At that point, I caught a glimpse of movement out of the corner of my eye and had a rush of embarrassment. If that was Luca coming along, it was not going to look good if he'd caught me talking to myself. I squinted into the darkness between the Math and Science buildings, expecting Loco to emerge. But instead of Loco, I could just make out a much shorter guy wearing what looked like a suit jacket and a scarf. He had a cellphone to his ear, and he was facing my way.

For a moment, he stayed like that, and then he turned his back quickly and shielded the phone. It was a strange, suspicious action, and I felt a touch of cold.

He's probably just trying to get out of the wind, I thought. And in fairness, the buildings of MIT seem to have a unique capacity for funnelling wind through them. An otherwise calm day can still produce a vortex that was hard to walk against in certain places on campus.

But I still felt uneasy. Maybe it was too much violence in the last twenty-four hours, or maybe it was the memory of that cold gaze through the car window. Whether it was rational or not, I could feel adrenaline kicking in.

I looked around for Luca, feeling a very old-fashioned kind-of need for the big-tough-guy in my life to swagger up and protect me. But instead of Luca, coming the other way towards the courtyard were three figures I didn't recognise from their unclear outlines, one of them a tall, slim girl with her hair piled on her head in a bun; the second a massive, thick-set guy who looked like he was a bouncer in a really rough club; and the third a medium-height guy with not a lot of hair.

They absolutely did not look like they belonged on campus, and they absolutely looked like they were walking my way.

Shit.

I scrambled off the picnic bench and hot-footed it across the courtyard, feeling unbelievably grateful that the nice boots I'd put on the night before were pretty good for jogging in. For some reason I couldn't bring myself to all-out sprint, though. I guess in the back of my mind was a suspicion that I was just being jumpy. So I did an awkward run-walk over to the Math building and bundled inside as quickly as I could.

The building was still as empty as it had been when I left,

the bright lights of the entrance-hall the only sign that it hadn't shut down for the holiday season. I thought, briefly, about running upstairs and trying to search people's offices. But I had no clue if any of the lecturers were around, and I didn't think they'd be much good against three possible drug-thugs either.

What I did have in my favour was a swipe-card for the computer lab. With the door locked behind me, they weren't going to be able to walk straight in and off me. It also bought me time to work out whether they were really after me, or I was just being a moron.

I looked over my shoulder as I swiped my card, but there was no sign of them yet. I ducked inside and closed the door, quietly. For good measure, I switched off the lights so that nothing shone through the small glass window in the door, and then I flattened myself against the wall and waited.

It didn't take long to have my worst suspicions confirmed. There was a muffled squeak from the outside door, and then quiet footsteps.

I heard the quiet mutter of a man's voice, and then the girl answering. Her voice was louder, energetic and modulated so that I could hear it through the door as she said, "I don't know. I only know she does math."

There was a twisting, awful feeling in my stomach. I recognised that voice, with its vitality, and its hint of Italian colouring the Boston accent. I'd heard quite a bit of it whilst she'd been all over Luca in her dad's Italian restaurant.

Rita? What the hell?

25

UNCOMFORTABLE TRUTHS

As the conversation continued without any input from the girl, I started to wonder if I was just going crazy. Was I just imagining things because I was essentially jealous?

But her figure had been right, too. Tall and really well put together. Her hair had been dark, and she'd moved in the same way I remembered Rita gliding over to Luca. There couldn't be too stunners like that out there who knew something about me, could there?

So maybe she knew them, too. Maybe her apparent interest in Luca was really to do with watching him on behalf of some of Rhett's friends. Which sounded all a little bit conspiracy-theory to me. But why else was she here looking for me with a couple of heavies?

I jumped as someone tried the handle of the computer-lab door. I held my breath as I heard a louder male voice.

"No lights on."

Of course, my phone chose that moment to issue a cheery chirp, announcing a text message.

Shit, shit, shit.

And then I heard another voice, which initially flooded me with relief.

"Can I help you?"

It was Eva Lang, my beloved math tutor. The building hadn't been empty after all. I risked a glance out of the window and saw her on the stairs, looming like some slightly middle-aged guardian angel.

"Sorry?" one of the men said.

"I asked if I could help you."

"No... No, we were just..."

"Were you looking for a friend? Because there aren't any students left this evening."

I got moved around a little and got a proper look at the guys outside while their attention was on Eva. The big one was doing the talking. He looked like an uglier version of Jason Statham and he spoke like he had a bad head-cold.

"We're waiting for someone."

Eva gave him a level look. "It could be a long wait. Security will be here to lock this place in about five minutes."

I glanced back at the big guy. He was staring right back at Eva like she was some kind of insect. Quite suddenly, I felt afraid instead of relieved. She was one defenceless person against two heavies and whatever Rita was. If they'd come to do something bad to me, would they see her as just another casualty?

My heart was in my throat somewhere as he stood stock-still, and then said quietly, "OK. Guess we'll catch her another time."

It was only as they started to leave and my breathing returned that I remembered that Luca would be out there by now, waiting for me.

I pulled out my cell-phone. The text had been from him:

Not to hassle you or anything, but I could probably eat about three of you right now I'm that hungry. Meet me in the Sports Cafe and I'll grab a burger xx

I typed back a quick and shaky:

Stay in the cafe - on my way. x

I sent it, and then counted to a hundred while I waited for the three of them to be well and truly gone. I still opened the door as quietly as possible, peering out toward the entrance which was thankfully empty. It looked dark and intimidating out beyond the doors, though, and I wondered if I could back down on my text and ask Luca to come back out here in ten minutes.

"Working in the dark?"

I must have lost a good year off my life with the shock the voice gave me. I'd just assumed that Eva had left, but she was standing behind the reception-desk, apparently looking for something in some papers. I was glad she wasn't making eye-contact.

My mouth was so dry that I couldn't get actual words out in reply. Not that I knew what to say anyway.

"I think some of your friends were looking for you," she went on.

I shook my head, and croaked, "Not friends."

She nodded her head, slowly. "I admit I couldn't see you four having coffee together. I've already called the security guard over. Maybe you should hang around here until he arrives."

I nodded, and waited with dread for her to ask me something, but she kept on hunting through those papers. In the end, it was my own desire to talk to someone that made me say, "It's not me they're looking for, really. It's - well, my boyfriend, I guess, but it's not even him really." She looked up at me, consideringly. "I didn't think you were the type."

"What type?"

"The type who's only into men who are bad news."

For some reason I found myself blushing. "I'm not. He's not

bad news at all, is the worst thing about it. His brother's in trouble, and he tried to help."

Eva gave a very slow nod, and then sighed. "You know, there's trouble and there's trouble, and at least one of those looked like the kind that needs the law getting involved. You need to talk to this boyfriend, and tell him he's not an action hero."

I smiled in spite of myself. "I'll try. And he's definitely got the wrong name for an action-hero."

The door squeaked open, letting in one of the friendlier security-guys from the gate.

"Am I walking you ladies somewhere?" he asked, and for once his slightly patronising air was nothing but reassuring.

I got them to walk me to the Sports Center, even though I really didn't want Eva catching sight of Loco. I knew she would be thinking badly of him, and it made me wince. I knew exactly why she was thinking like she did, and I knew he didn't deserve it.

The whole thought-process made me feel exactly like a dumb teenager all over again, the kind who defends her no-good boyfriend and believes that nobody understands him. And then I felt even more like a teenager when Luca glanced up from a table and my legs went a little bit useless.

"Hey, Taylor," he said, giving me a small, tired smile. "Did you start coding again and forget all about me?"

I thought about those three coming to find me and tried to smile at him. I did my best to wak over normally and I gave him a hug where he sat. My arms were shaking so much that he clearly felt it, and stood with a frown.

"What's up?"

I had one of those weird moments when I tried to talk, but instead ended up fighting not to cry. To hide the humiliation, I buried my head against his shoulder and gave him a firm squeeze. It was easier to swallow it down and talk when not looking at him.

"Slight problem with some people we almost know," I said. "Looks like some associates of Rhett's were looking for me."

He drew back from me, in obvious shock. "Are you serious?"

I nodded, and looked away from his gaze to try and keep on holding it together.

"How did they know about you?"

"I think you have a slight informant problem," I said, hating that I had to tell him. "You know that girl from the restaurant? Rita? She was with them."

I made some eye-contact with him again, and it was the most uncomfortable thing seeing him fight not to believe me.

"Rita? Seriously? What are - Are you sure? I don't think she's got anything to do with those guys. She hasn't even been here for ages."

I nodded at him. "I saw her, too. I'm pretty positive. She just seemed to know I did Math here. Do you think she knew that?"

There was a pause, and then, slowly, Loco nodded. "She messaged after you left the restaurant. She was - she was wondering if everything was ok. I said yes, fine, that something had come up, that you were an impulsive math genius and it wasn't a worry. We - we chatted a bit about you. But I don't-"

He shook his head, trying to deny it again.

"Maybe you need to talk to her," I said, despite hating the idea of him going anywhere near her.

"Yeah, maybe I do."

I let him put his arm around me but we walked in silence out of the cafe, his burger forgotten on the table. I didn't know if I was imagining waves of distrust coming off him, but it made me feel pretty terrible.

"Hey," I said to him, as we reached the parking-lot and he

opened up his beat-up old car. "I hope it turns out to be ok. I didn't - I don't want to mess things up with your friends."

He shook his head, and gave me a grin as he pulled me gently toward him. "Yeah, you're so inconsiderate, being hunted down by my people and some of my brother's drug-dealing friends." He gave me a light kiss on the lips. "Sorry, I'm probably coming across all angry. But literally none of it is directed at you. I'm just trying to find a scenario in all this where it's nothing more a mistake, and hoping that I haven't just dragged you into a mess. K?"

"I'm glad," I said, enjoying the hug he gave me more now. "Cos I hate having to be angry back. It's so tiring."

I felt about a thousand times better as we drove away, but there was still a part of me that was terrified about Rita convincing him I'd made it all up, and another part of me that was more normally afraid of being in danger. On the plus side of it all, I had absolutely no space to indulge in the more regular kind-of worry about losing Luca. If I was being positive about the current threat-to-my-life, it was at least a little different.

26

THE SMALLEST OF BETRAYALS

It was not a good journey. Luca was all but silent, clearly going over and over things in his mind and not finding any particularly nice conclusions. I went through about five cycles of doubt, convincing myself that I had been wrong about it being Rita, and then that I'd misunderstood somehow. But the truth of my fear was still there in the jittery feeling that was running through me, and I was dreading having the danger I'd been in confirmed too.

In the end, at the point where we'd crossed the bridge into Chelsea, I made a disgusted noise at myself, and inwardly told myself to stop it. Luca focused on me, and reached out with his right hand to squeeze my leg.

"We'll sort this out," he said, and gave me a half-smile. "It's my mess, not yours."

"It's our mess," I said, firmly, and grabbed his hand. "Joint custody of the mess."

"Dammit, does that mean I only get the mess every other weekend?"

"Yeah, but you can meet it from school half the week."

He nodded. "OK. I can deal with that as long as I can take it to practice and get it a shirt with my name on. Our mess, then." And he kissed my hand at the same moment I caught sight of a tall figure with piled-up hair exiting a car up ahead.

"Slow up," I said, urgently, and Luca did better than that by pulling the car off the road and into the entrance to a run-down parking lot that edged by bent wire fencing.

"So that was Rita," he said, with a slight crack to his voice. I felt sorry for him. He hadn't wanted it to be her. I could understand him wishing I'd been wrong.

"Yeah, it was," I said. "Guess they gave her a ride home."

He found a space in the far corner of the parking lot, and we both got out. Luca looked at me like he was going to make me stay, and then decided to keep quiet. Which was wise, given how angry all the adrenalin was making me feel right then.

I followed him back towards the street, and he did a surprisingly good job of walking casually out onto the sidewalk with his cell-phone out, letting him keep his head down whilst he glanced up under his still-damp hair.

I waited for him to nod before going to join him. The car was gone, and the sidewalk outside the restaurant we had visited - what, a few days ago? Or years and years ago? I wasn't sure - was empty. I was glad of the way he pulled me firmly towards him and kept his arm there as we walked the few yards to the restaurant. It helped me keep myself together.

"You don't want to go and talk to her first, do you?" I asked, as we drew nearer.

Luca frowned. "Why would I want to do that?"

"I just figure... it's easier on her."

He thought it through momentarily before shaking his head.

"I'm not going in there without showing her that I'm with you, even if that does make it harder on her. Whatever she's done, it wasn't a good thing, and it could have pretty easily have gotten you hurt. I think she's given away her rights to the baby treatment, don't you?"

And then we were inside the busy restaurant, before I could reply.

Rita was the near side of the bar, adjusting her hair while she talked to her father, her long back to us. I saw Alfredo's face when he saw us, and it was half defiant, half guilty. He knew what Rita had been doing.

"Luca," he said, and glanced at me. "I'm - glad to see you. I think we need to talk."

Rita was pale as she turned around. I couldn't help feeling sorry for her. Really, actively sorry. She looked close to crying, and she tried her hardest not to look at me.

What a goddamn mess, I thought.

"Yes, we do," Luca said, drawing me towards the hatch in the bar and not meeting Rita's anxious gaze.

"I think... it would be better if we did it alone," Alfredo said, looking at me with a look that was as cold as anything I could remember. Was this what they were really like, these friends of Loco's?

And then I began to have a suspicion that I knew what was going on here.

"We're all going to talk, openly," Luca said, firmly, and gestured for me to go ahead of him behind the bar. I didn't know where I was going after that, but Luca leaned forward to push open the door to the kitchen and I shuffled through. This was about the most awkward situation I could remember being in. It even beat that time my Mom dropped into conversation with the boy I had a crush on in the third grade that I had she recognised him from the picture on my computer. Which was something I'd thought would never happen. I didn't know if I wanted to kiss Loco full on the mouth or punch him right then.

The kitchen was hot and busy, with one waiter and a chef in

the midst of a slanging-match in Italian. I wondered if we were going to try and talk here, but Luca led me past the steam and the amazing smells to a small door. There was a table just outside covered by a porch, which must have been where the staff took their breaks to eat or read. At the moment it was empty except for a grubby ash-tray in the middle.

I took a chair and sat, feeling like it was me who had to defend myself here. Alfredo sat with a sigh, and Luca waited for Rita to come outside, her body language reluctant, and then held out a hand to the third chair. She pulled it out quickly, making it clatter on the brick paving, and sat without looking at him again.

It was a good thing Luca sat beside me and squeezed my leg firmly before he started. I was feeling a little bit like I might puke from a mixture of adrenalin, fear and awkwardness.

"What were you doing this evening, Rita?" Luca asked, straight off. I could hear the anger in his voice, the sense of betrayal, and I saw from the way she flinched that she could, too.

"Now look," Alfredo interrupted, holding out a hand. "Before you start attacking my daughter, you need to know a few things. We had a visit from a couple of cops earlier today. They told us that this young woman is known to them." He pointed at me with a jab, a chain bracelet on his wrist clanking as he did it. "Which I am guessing you must know too."

Luca was almost comically shocked for a moment, and then shook his head, slowly. "She isn't known to the police, Alfredo."

"They told us everything," Rita said suddenly, in a rush. "They told us about and how you've been trying to help her. I know it's easy for people to prey on someone like you, Luca, because you're so warm-hearted, but you have to look out for yourself. You can't get dragged into this. You're on a sports' scholarship. If they get even a sniff of drugs..."

"Wait, what?"

I felt even more sick as Luca looked over at me with wide eyes, but then he cracked a smile, which turned into real, unexpected laughter.

"They told you she had a drug habit? And you believed them?"

Rita looked both hurt and confused. "They were cops, Luca."

"Rita, those guys would run a mile if they saw a cop. Did you really think they looked legit?"

"Luca-"

"Cally's only habit is telling people to take a hike a bit too quickly," he interrupted her. "And I'm ok with that. Even if she does it to me someday, which I really hope she won't. I mean, I won't be ok with it. I'll be pissed off and hurt. But I'll understand."

I could see the battle in Rita. She was looking from one to the other of us, not really wanting to believe him.

"I'm sorry they lied to you," I said, quietly. "But I don't have any connection to any kind of drugs that aren't in coffee and occasionally glasses of wine. Really."

"Whereas those guys," Luca said, with feeling, "those guys you sold out to without asking, are mired in that world and have dragged by brother into it. They didn't want to arrest Cally, they wanted to hurt her. If you'd led them to her, she might be at the bottom of the Charles by now."

Alfredo stood, suddenly.

"Do not talk to her like that," Rita's father said, "when she has tried to help you. Even if you are right-"

"All right, all right. I shouldn't attack either of you, I'm sorry," Luca said, making an effort to calm down. "I'm just - I guess I'm angry at the possible consequences, and I'm angry that you didn't talk to me about it first. I know it came from a place of caring about me, but why didn't you talk to me?"

Rita's eyes started to ooze large tears.

"Because I thought I'd lost you," she said, and then she stood and walked unsteadily to the door. She disappeared into the restaurant, and Luca's face was torn.

"Should I go after her?" he asked Alfredo.

"No," her father said, waving a hand and scowling. "Not now. Not while you're here with Cally." He glanced at me, and then sighed. "I hate to ask - like this, but - you're sure?"

"I'm sure," Luca said. "They're stooges of Axel's ex-boyfriend. He... he got into a mess because he was naive, and now they want money from him. They didn't like me telling them no, and stepping in to protect him. It's my screw-up, and Cally's the one suffering for it."

Alfredo looked steadily at him, and then sighed.

"So you're in trouble? You need help? My brother..."

Luca shook his head, rapidly.

"Thank you. But I need to deal with this myself. I can't involve you, or Rita. They'd know where to find you both, and I'm not ok with that."

Alfredo sighed again.

"OK. You know you can ask me if - you know that we are here for you."

Luca nodded, and squeezed my hand absently. I saw Alfredo's eyes follow the gesture, and the sadness in his expression.

"Will Rita - she'll be ok?" Luca asked.

"Of course she will," Alfredo said.

Luca nodded, and then started to get up. We left together, hand in hand. As I reached the door to the restaurant, I glanced back at Alfredo, who was sitting dejectedly at the table.

"I'm sorry," I said.

He looked up at me, startled. "What do you have to be sorry about? It is none of it your fault. I hope that - I hope you remain safe."

I nodded, and followed Luca.

There was no sign of Rita in the kitchen or the restaurant, but Luca still waited until we were out on the sidewalk to hold me tightly to him and kiss me.

"I'm ok," I said, with a small smile, once he released me.

"I know, but - fuck. If they'd got you... if they'd hurt you..."

He kissed me again, and despite my attention initially being on the road behind him as I looked out for the heavies to come back, I pretty quickly forgot about everything apart from the feel of it.

He drew back mere inches, and said, "I'm not quite sure I can handle you being out of my life."

I felt a rush of hurt and fear that I tried very hard to repress.

"You know I'm not going anywhere," I said.

"But you have to. For now. You know that, don't you? Until it's safe. You have to."

I dug my fingers into the flesh of his back as I replied, without being able to look at him, "I know. I know."

27

THE HARDEST THING IS SAYING GO

I changed my flights that night. It meant calling Fernando up and lying to him about having finished my coding project and being lonely. There was no way I had enough in my account to cover a twelve-hundred-dollar last-minute trip in the holiday season, and I needed him to step in.

"Are you sure you don't mind?" I said to him, for about the tenth time, as he told me the money had been transferred.

"Of course I don't," he said, with all the warmth that I'd always liked in him so much. "You have no idea how upset your mother's been about you not being home earlier. And I miss you sometimes, too. So, you know, it's not just about getting her to shut up about it."

I laughed, almost disappointed that this was really happening. I'd even been granted an extension on my coding project, so there was no excuse any more.

"You want me to pick you up from the airport?" Fernando asked, before ringing off.

"Actually - that'd be great."

The idea of arriving alone and taking the train out to

Marlbro town was miserable. It was going to take Fernando an hour to drive each way, but the idea of being cushioned in his gorgeous Lamborghini gave the trip a little something to look forward to.

"What's the flight number?"

Heavy-hearted, I opened my laptop and checked the page I already had up.

"It's AA268."

"I'll be there. Can't wait."

There were two muffled clicks and then he was gone. Luca was already sliding his arms around me and although I can remember the sound now, right then it was unimportant. I was looking at that bright, unforgiving screen, and there was nothing for it but to click the "Purchase" button and accept that I was going.

"You want to catch a movie or something while we get everything packed up?" he murmured, once I'd paid the breathtakingly large amount of money for the flights and gone through the online check-in.

"No," I said, leaning back into him. "Can we just talk? About your brother? And about, I don't know... all the stupid things you used to do when you were young?"

"Umm, we only have until the morning..."

Somehow I managed to laugh at it, and to keep laughing while I packed away my worldly belongings.

I don't want to go. I don't want to go.

It was a little mantra in my head, and it only got drowned out by a stream of inane, cheerful chatter that I somehow kept up the whole way to the airport.

Looking back on it, I feel like I might have known something. I was never one for premonitions, but most of my certainties about the world had been overturned by the crazy stuff I could do, and then by the craziness Luca did. Maybe I did know. Or maybe I was just too used to losing people.

Whatever the reason, I was trying so hard to hold in a wave of sadness and fear that I didn't have room for silence. If I'd stopped with my monologue about Christmas and my Mom and Fernando and the flight, I'd have started choking on tears. I'd have begged Loco not to make me leave him. And I might have let him thaw me out a little, but I wasn't going to come across as needy. No I was not.

He parked up high up in the multi-storey lot and walked with me all the way to the terminal. He was quiet, watching my face and smiling slightly, but his arm never left its place around me, and when we finally arrived in the bright, busy airport, he turned towards me and gave me a kiss so fierce it was hard to breathe.

I still sort-of hated him for the way he made me want to melt into him; for the way I would forget everything; for the sigh of desire that escaped me pretty much every time. I let go of my bags and wrapped myself around him, letting him muss up my hair with one hand and push my sweater up with the other, and not caring.

I don't know who went back for more kisses, him or me, but it seemed like it couldn't stop. They punctuated our few words.

"Message me when you land."

"OK. Will you - let me know what happens? Everything?"

"I promise. Everything I eat, and every piece of crap I watch on TV."

"Good. And, you know... any drug dealers who may or may not come after you."

He smiled at me, close-up, his green eyes on me. Then he leaned his forehead against mine and for a few moments he rocked us both to a music I couldn't hear.

"I'm going to miss you, Ms. Taylor."

"I guess I might miss you too."

I thought about saying more, but that awful lump in my throat was growing, and I knew I had to go if I was going to hold it in.

I let go of him, and it made me feel somehow better and sadder that he tried to hold on for a moment before he stepped back.

I made it to the security line without quite breaking down, but I was losing the room a little as my eyes filled up.

"Hey, Cally!" he called out, and I turned, seeing a fragmented version of him.

"What?"

"Do I get a Christmas present?"

"Only if you don't get dead, ok?"

He laughed, still not leaving, and looking so hot and so vulnerable just then in the middle of all that light and hard, reflective floor that I couldn't stand it.

"Don't you have someplace to be?" I called, with a smile.

He sighed. "I guess."

And then he ran over, ducked under the tape into the queue and straightened in front of me. I was already crying by the time he kissed me, but when he drew away from me his eyes were as wet as mine.

"Pussy," I muttered, and he gave a one-shouldered shrug and a half-smile and then, finally, left. It took all my self-control and steady breathing not to lose the fragile control I had on my feelings towards him.

"He'll be ok," I said, out loud, and found myself not caring at all that I was crying and talking to myself in front of a line of strangers.

Maybe if I hadn't been crying so hard, I would have seen them coming. Maybe I could have ducked aside, or pushed towards the security guys on the desk. But as it was, there was no warning until someone jostled into me, and I felt something uncomfortable dig into my side.

"Step out of the queue."

It was a quiet voice, but the kind of voice that knew it was going to be obeyed. I was almost moving before I'd had a chance to think, and then when I paused to think, I realised that what was digging into me was a knife. I only hesitated long enough to see that it was the smaller guy who'd followed me into the Math department. The bright light was shining off his slightly-balding head, and meeting his eyes was like the opposite of looking at Luca. Where those green eyes had been full of communication and emotion and feeling, this guy was absolutely calm, and flat, and unconcerned. It scared the hell out of me.

I ducked under the tape while he held it up for me. I almost walked off without my suitcase, but he gave a flicker of a smile.

"Don't forget your case, darling."

I think that was worse than the order and the knife together. That calm pretence for everyone else in the queue, and the word "darling" used by a man who I was willing to bet had not a shred of empathy.

By the time I'd straightened up from dragging my case out from the line after me, he had managed to manoeuvre himself so that the knife was back against my ribs. I couldn't even see it myself, so there was no way anyone else was going to see and help me.

"Walk," he said, quietly, and I did it, the tears in my eyes beginning to clear. There were people waiting: two of them, one small and one large.

It was like an out-of-body-experience as I walked over to them. Fear is a strange thing when it's that intense. Nothing is real, and you think you might just stop breathing or functioning.

Like it can't go on. But each second is followed by another, and you're still there, and still afraid.

"Hello, dearest," Rhett said to me as I grew close enough to make him out. He smiled that blank, lizard-smile of his, but there was a flicker to it, and I realised that he was scared, too. "Let's go and see a friend of mine."

28

A DANGEROUS MAN

It's strange how slowly I started being able to think again. I mean, I'm not actually stupid, despite a lot of my behaviour. I'm supposed to be pretty smart. And yet I don't think anything that could be classified a thought crossed my mind for minutes.

I think it was Rhett's fear that changed things. It altered the situation from them all being simply Bad Guys to there being one Bad Guy I really had to worry about. And then things started whirring and clicking, and I realised that they were taking me with the single purpose of getting at Luca. This had nothing to do with me except that he cared about me. It was why they'd come after me, thanks to Rita's willingness to believe them.

And I was in a crowded airport. They weren't going to stab me here, in front of hundreds of people. Not with CCTV and security guards scattered around the place.

So I stopped in front of Rhett and said, "No."

His expression didn't change, it just froze in place for several seconds while I tried to go on thinking.

"You don't have any choice, dearest."

The bald guy made the point a little clearer by digging the knife into me until I knew it had pierced my sweater and shirt and cut into my skin. I tried to flinch away but he was holding onto me too tightly.

Come on. Think. Think.

What do they want? What can you do?

"What is wrong with you?" I asked, rounding on him. "I'm so sick of all this bullshit! I don't want anything to do with you or him. He's a cheating asshole and good riddance to him."

When I turned back to him, I saw a flicker of something on Rhett's face. It was an uptick in the fear. I tried not to look anything but upset and angry as he watched me, trying to work out if I was telling the truth; if I really didn't mean all that much to Loco.

My phone buzzed, and his eyes narrowed, consideringly.

Shit. Please just let it be Mom.

My hand went to my pocket, but the bald guy had my phone in his hand already. I didn't even have a proper lock-screen, so he swiped it open, and then held it out to me, expressionlessly.

It was the kind of text that would have brought a warm, squishy kind of feeling to my insides and made me smile in an annoying way in any other circumstances.

I THINK **you forgot to text and tell me you miss me already. I mean, just commenting and all.x**

"Doesn't sound like a cheating asshole to me."

I looked up at him, out of ideas, and then beyond him, to where a pair of Massachusetts State Troopers were wandering through the airport.

"Help-"

Was what I wanted to say as I lunged forward, but the bald guy grabbed me so hard towards him that my nose slammed into his shoulder. I couldn't see anything, but I could smell him. A horrible, slightly sour smell as if he hadn't washed his clothes quite enough or had sweated in them too much. And then suddenly there was something else in my face, something whitish, and I thought they were trying to choke me with it. I fought, but my vision and my balance started going and I was falling somewhere, shouting Loco's name for all I was worth.

I can't have been out for that long. I was hazy when I woke up, but with a memory of where I'd been, and what had been happening, and I tried to scrabble from what felt like half-lying to standing.

It didn't work. My arms and legs weren't quite under my control and my head thumped into something before I fell sideways. Which was when I realised I was in a car, before my eyes had really booted back up again.

A grip like a wrench came round my wrist, and I heard a terse order to "Sit still!" Which by that point I'd realised I had to do. I was too dizzy and the car was moving too fast for anything else.

So I sat, and gradually worked out that the bald guy was next to me, holding my arm; that the huge guy who'd come looking for me with Rita was driving; and that Rhett was next to him. Smarmy little Rhett was turning to look out of the window, trying to look casual, but I could see the way his fingers were tapping on the dash in little off-beat staccatos, and he shifted in his seat every few seconds. I'd been right about him being scared.

It was an expensive car. The seats were real, soft leather in dark grey and it moved smoothly even at speed. The fear had kicked right back in, and I had such an intense moment of longing for Luca's beat-up old motor instead that it felt like a pain in my stomach.

I remembered my cell-phone, and went to get it out with my free hand. It wasn't there, of course.

"Where's my phone?" I asked, not really expecting them to answer. But to my surprise, the bald guy pulled it out of his own pocket without letting go of my wrist and waved it at me.

"We needed it to send your boyfriend a little message."

I felt cold. Worse than cold. I'd already let them use me to get to him.

"What did you say?" I whispered.

"To wait until we called him. I think we got his attention."

I imagined Luca panicking. I imagined him angry, and raging, and as afraid as I was.

I imagined him wanting to bring down punishment on all of them. I wanted to believe that it would work, but I wasn't even sure it was possible on so many people. And I was with them. Could he control it enough to make sure I didn't get hurt? Would he even risk it? And that was assuming they didn't do anything to me before he even got there, which was terrifying in itself.

I was so wrapped up in stressing myself out over it that it didn't even occur to me to work out where we were driving to. Not until we pulled down an alleyway I half recognised and then through an open pair of gates into a tiny enclosed courtyard. It was surrounded by a tall building quite cheerfully painted in pale blue, which was totally out of step with the heavies in the car with me.

"Out you get," the bald guy said, reaching across to open my door.

I gave serious thought to running. I'm not exactly slow, and with the amount of extra weight the big guy in the front was carrying, I doubted he'd be able to catch me before I made it out onto the road. Which always left the prospect of them shooting me in the back, but I was almost willing to gamble on being worth more to them as a living hostage than as a dead one.

But even as I was climbing out of the car and bracing myself to push off it, the gates closed with a quiet metallic noise. There was no way I could scale those before someone grabbed me. I was here with them, wherever here was.

The big guy was out of the car now, too. I nodded at him as he gestured ahead of him, towards a stone staircase leading to a white-painted door. I hoped if I went quietly enough that there would be no manhandling.

Rhett was ahead of me going upwards, and he let himself in with a swipe-card that reminded me of the ones at MIT. This whole place was a jumble of different things. Old building, pastel colours, modern technology... and gangsters.

The interior was no less surprising. I'd been expecting from the windowless courtyard to step into darkness. But through the door was a huge, opened-out hallway with a glass ceiling maybe three floors above and big windows ahead with a view of trees and a row of buildings behind them. It was a spare place, but where it was furnished, it was lush with a thick rug that begged to have your hands run through it, and a gorgeous scarlet curtains. It was like some kind of a hidden boutique hotel, and I didn't know what to make of it.

Rhett had turned towards a delicately-fashioned spiral staircase, and we climbed up to a suspended floor above, where I had a glimpse of a gleaming kitchen and a large dining-table, and then on up to another. This one was closed off by a wall painted in pale yellow, and there was a plain wooden door set into it.

Rhett glanced at me, trying to smile smugly. But there was more tension in him than ever and it was actually a lot more effective at giving me an extra dose of shit-scared than any sneer would have been.

He rapped on the door.

For a good five seconds there was no reply. It was like waiting for the result of a doctor's scan, or an exam result, only a million times worse. Right then I would have preferred to lose another friend than walk in through that door.

But not Luca, I thought, and it was a weird kind of strength to realise that. I'd sooner walk in than lose him.

And then without any preceding sounds, the door clicked open, and swung silently inwards. Rhett jumped more than I did, and then gestured to me to walk ahead of him, his hand going up to straighten his hair nervously.

I'm going to stop this somehow, I told myself, as I stepped forwards. It was pretty much the only way I could convince myself to go inside. I'm going to stop them from hurting Luca.

And then I was inside, in another brightly-lit room with a view out over greenery and a row of apartments. I suddenly realised where we were. This was Commonwealth Avenue. Rhett's drug-dealing boss had a house - probably two houses together gutted and rebuilt, looking at the size of it all - on the beautiful main street that ran through the heart of the city. He was there in plain sight.

And plain to my sight, too, and he wasn't even close to what I'd expected.

It was partly that he was young. I'd say my age or a little older. For some reason that didn't work with a drug lord. He should have been somewhere in his fifties or sixties, and running to fat, with rings on his fingers and a cigar.

This guy looked like he didn't touch tobacco. Or anything else drug-related for that matter. He was lean and healthy-looking, and he was sitting in front of a laptop at a glass desk, not with the calculated lounge of the master-criminal but with the intent interest of someone at work.

I had a few moments to simply look at him, at the slightly

long dark hair that flopped artfully into his eyes, and the thick-rimmed black glasses he wore. I couldn't place his ethnicity exactly, but there was something Eastern in the skin-tone, the high cheekbones and the darkness of his eyes.

When he looked up at me it was with curiosity, and appraisal. There was no sinister smile, and no air of victory. And yet I could feel fear coming off Rhett in waves.

"Thank you, Rhett," he said, quietly.

"Mr. Jeroniri," Rhett said, and it sounded strange addressed to a younger man, that respectful tone.

"You have her cell-phone?"

The bald guy stepped up from behind me, making me jump, and placed it carefully on the glass desk.

Mr. Jeroniri glanced down at it, and he sighed.

"I don't like this way of doing things," he said, his voice light and sounding well-educated East-Coast through and through. "I suppose you know that Rhett here engaged Axel Veste to deliver a package for me?"

I nodded, guessing there was no reason to deny it.

"I hoped, when the package was not delivered, that we could make simple amends. I much prefer a financial solution to a physical one. This is, after all, a business."

There was a brief chime that sounded like an email alert, and he glanced at the computer-screen, and then back at me.

"But Axel's brother has made things difficult. Two of my own want blood for what he did. One for the injury done to him, and one for his own brother."

I remembered the two guys outside the nightclub, and I wanted to tell him that wasn't fair. Luca had just protected himself, and his brother. But I was wary of arguing, and of making him angry. I had to figure this all out somehow, and making him angry wouldn't help me.

"And I must be seen to be fair to my own. Fair - and firm."

I suddenly caught a trace of the threat that Rhett seemed to feel. His gaze was steady and unflinching and almost fractionally sympathetic. Which for some reason made it all much, much worse.

"I had hoped that bringing in the younger brother would bring in the older," he went on. "But Axel has done an effective job of disappearing, and there is no good in a display of force if it is slow and laboured. Which is where you come in."

I shook my head, but he nodded in response.

"You're going to call Luca, and tell him exactly what I ask you to. And then we will all of us vanish out of your life like a bad dream. If you don't - it will be you who vanishes, Miss Taylor."

I couldn't think then. I could see the very real threat of death looking at me, but my mind wouldn't go anywhere except to the same place. Over, and over, and over it told me no. I wouldn't help them to hurt him. I wouldn't.

"Then I'll have to vanish," I whispered.

Mr. Jeroniri frowned at me, lines briefly appearing behind his strands of hair.

"You need to think very carefully about this," he said. "I am not naturally violent, but I have removed people from my path before. I wouldn't hesitate. And I will get to Luca somehow, with or without your help. By making a show, all you're going to do is hurt him the worse before we get to him. Send him mad with guilt. Is that what you want?"

I couldn't think of anything to say, and so I kept my mouth shut, ashamed of the way my lips were shaking. The absolute silence was interrupted only by another chime on the laptop, and the boy in front of me - I couldn't think of him as a man even while he told me he would have me killed - glanced over.

And then he gave me a small smile, and a nod.

"One wishes to vanish, and another one appears."

I must have looked as lost as I felt, and so Mr. Jeroniri explained in careful terms to me.

"Axel has turned up, right here in Boston, and is now with my men. Which means it's time you made a phone-call, Miss Taylor."

29

WHEN THINGS ARE STARTING TO GO WRONG

My hands were shaking like some kind of frightened animal as I dialled Luca's number. I told myself I was just buying time while I thought my way out of this. I told myself I wasn't betraying him, because he already knew that they had me.

It didn't matter what I told myself. I felt like Judas as the single ring went through to his cell-phone. He picked up quickly enough that I knew he'd been waiting with his thumb on the button.

"Cally." His voice didn't sound like him. It sounded at once harsher, and more vulnerable. It sounded like they'd already done something terrible to him before they'd even touched him.

"Luca, I'm sorry." I wanted to say it first, while I had the chance. I was sorry. Heart-achingly sorry. If I'd made it through security, he could have picked them off one by one using a power they didn't know he had. He would be safe.

"Don't say that. Are you all right?"

"Yes. Yes, but they say - they say they have Axel too. That he came back. Brandon said he needed him and..."

There wasn't a lot else to say about it. I knew he would want to smack Axel in the face as much as I did; and we were in agreement that Brandon was a waste of space. None of it needed saying between us.

There were two hurried breaths into the mouthpiece, breaths I could almost feel on my skin, and then he said, "OK. You believe them?"

I glanced up at Mr. Jeroniri, the boy with the laptop, and then said, "Yes, I do."

"What do they want?"

"For you to go to an address." The boy drug-lord passed a piece of paper across the table, with a scratchy handwritten note. It was an industrial unit off the Interstate. Out of town, and out of the way. I could hear the fear in my voice as I read it out to him. "Mr. Jeroniri wants you to know that he will bring me and your brother there, and that we'll be free to go in exchange for you coming to talk to him."

"I guess he's heard what a good conversationalist I am," Loco said, and I gave a half-desperate laugh.

"I guess he has. He says that you have his word that he will release us if you arrive there and hand yourself over, and that his word means a great deal to him."

"I'm assuming there are lots of conditions about not bringing the cops, or anyone else."

"Yes."

I didn't need to say that it hadn't surprised me. Or that I was scared.

"It'll be ok," he said, quietly. I could feel my eyes stinging. There was none of the certainty in his voice that he'd had about us, and our future together. He was as scared as I was.

"Of course it will," I said, lying as hard in return. And then, quickly, as I could see the bald guy holding his hand out for my cell-phone, "I did miss you. I do miss you. You can have a million texts by way of apology. Just..."

I broke off, because I couldn't say in front of the listening men, Just live. Please, please, just live.

He gave a gentle but hoarse laugh into my ear.

"I'll take that. Tell them I'm on my way."

"I will."

After I hung up, I had to close my eyes and squeeze my hands into fists for a moment just to stop the fear and the sadness taking over. I felt the phone being tugged out of my hand by the bald guy, and fought the urge to clutch onto it, just because it was my one contact with Luca.

"Has he agreed?" Jeroniri asked.

I nodded, and with an effort opened my eyes again. "He says he's on his way."

"Thank you," the drug-lord said. He reached for his laptop and typed rapidly for a moment, before pushing it away again. "You may as well have a seat. This will take a little while."

I looked at him blankly, my brain not computing. "What will?"

"All of this... business. You'll be released once it's over. I meant it when I gave my word."

"But... Shouldn't we get going? To the warehouse or wherever it is?"

"We aren't going," Jeroniri explained, quite gently. "It's too complex setting up a hostage situation, and too likely to end in disaster. Much safer and simpler to arrange for the men he has angered to... clear things up."

The blankness became an awful understanding.

"You're just going to let them pick him off?" I whispered. "You aren't even going to talk to him?"

Jeroniri sighed. "I told you I don't like this way of doing things. But Luca has angered the wrong people, and in so doing has become a threat to me. What has complicated the issue is that he seems to have an extraordinary ability to cover his tracks.

We've spent most of our resources since the nightclub incident trying to find him, and haven't sniffed even a trace. So it became imperative that he be forced into the open."

I shook my head at him, mutely for a few seconds, before I broke out with, "Please. Please don't. You can reason with him. He wants a quiet life, you just threatened his brother. Rhett and your associates were a danger to Axel. If you can sort that out, he won't bother you again."

"The situation with Axel can be regarded as closed," he said, turned to face his laptop and frowning briefly before typing again. His interest in me was gone, I could see. He was moving on to other business, no longer willing to talk. I could have grabbed him by the throat right then and squeezed until he choked. It was a terrifyingly strong emotion.

The bald guy grabbed my arm and pulled me over to the sofa. I fought for a moment but then realised that I wasn't going to be able to resist them using physical force. I needed another way.

I was shaking convulsively as I sat down, my mind spinning in circles. I had to force myself to breathe in and out just to begin thinking.

Come on. Come on! What can you do? What can you do?

If I could just warn Luca somehow. But although I knew I could be aware of him if I needed to, there was no way I could make him aware of me. I felt powerless, and wished intensely that I had his ability to create revenge instead of my own. It would have done so much more good.

But even thinking that produced a light in my mind.

You know what you can do.

I looked up, slowly, at Jeroniri. At his impassive face as he waited for them to kill Luca. That anger was still in me, but I pushed it away and focused on his slightly floppy hair for a moment.

He's just a boy. Just a boy playing games. A boy who is too smart for his own good, and has set up an empire he can't control.

And suddenly I saw the kid who had ended up here: the child who had no friends his own age; who spent hours on his computer, and began to realise that he could have power and influence in a virtual world; who began exchanging and trading and making contacts; who happened upon the most lucrative market of all, and began to become a drug-lord little by little.

And in spite of all this, I thought, *he's still alone.*

I could read the loneliness in him. I could read that the people he surrounded himself with were no more his friends than a pack of hungry wolves. I could read the ache to find someone to really talk to; someone who was smart and empathetic. Someone who might save him from himself.

And it was there. That magnetic pull. The feeling of two points moving together. It was extraordinarily strong in only a matter of moments, fuelled by the urgency of my need for it to happen. I put nothing in its way - I drew the feeling into me and felt the other point in this binary system moving towards us rapidly. They were close, and drawing closer all the time.

Quickly, I thought. *Quickly, quickly. Please. Luca doesn't have much time.*

There was suddenly a curious frown on Jeroniri's face, as if he could feel something. He glanced up at me, and gave me a speculative look.

I remembered, suddenly, Loco telling me he could feel what I'd done.

Oh god, please don't stop me doing this. They're so close. And you'll finally be happy.

I stared right back at him, unable to look away if I was going to keep that intense, magnetic draw going. I tried to tell him with my eyes that what I was doing was good. I tried to give him a sense that it would all be all right, now, and he wouldn't have to be lonely any more.

They're so close.

That other point was almost on us. They must have been in the building already, and coming up to this floor.

Come on! Come on!

Jeroniri's frown deepened, and he began to say, "Cooper, would you-"

A sharp tap came at the door.

Jeroniri pressed a button on his computer, distractedly, looking like he was bothered by what was happening. He began again, "Perhaps we should take Ms Taylor..."

But then the door opened, and into a glorious sliver of sunlight walked Jeroniri's soul-mate; the person he had been waiting all his life to find; a beautiful, slight, dark-haired Adonis.

I could feel my own mouth hanging open even while Jeroniri gaped at him.

Oh holy shit. Not Axel.

30

THERE IS ALWAYS SOMETHING WORSE

He's going to kill me. He's actually going to kill me.

Stupidly, it was the only thing I could think. I didn't mean Jeroniri the teenage-drug-lord, or any of his henchmen - I meant Luca. Because after all the conversations we'd had about Axel and how he deserved better and needed to be free of the world of drugs, I'd just paired him up for good with the biggest, baddest fish in that reeking pond.

I think even some of the stooges could see it. They didn't need my sense of my ability, or to know about it. They could tell from the way Axel stopped short, and Jeroniri rose from his chair.

The one behind Axel wasn't lucky enough to have worked it out. He gave the boy a shove, and Jeroniri's voice was suddenly like a whip-crack.

"Get your hands off him!"

There was a pulsing, tense silence. And then Jeroniri said, "I'm sorry that my associates aren't treating you with respect. It won't happen again."

He sat slowly and gestured to a chair by the wall. The bald guy close to me hurried to fetch it. It was the first real display of

Jeroniri's power, and of his potential to be angry, and it gave me a sense of grim satisfaction to see that it was now all in Axel's favour.

Axel moved in that dreamlike state that hits them all. He sat in front of Jeroniri, and he smiled at him. If the guy hadn't been a drug baron, it might have been heartwarming.

"Axel. I'm glad that I found you."

"Me too," Axel said, and Rhett looked sharply over at the bald guy, who seemed like he was determined not to react at this bizarre turn of events. Rhett didn't just look confused; he looked angry. Of course he did. Here was Axel, his fall-guy, suddenly being treated like royalty.

Stick that in your cocktail-maker and shake it, Rhett, I thought.

"I had lots of questions to ask you," Jeroniri said, leaning forward over his desk with a half-smile. "Rhett had me convinced that you were a thief."

Axel shook his head. "I was stolen from. And I don't think it was a coincidence. He used me because I was young and stupid, and it took a long time for me to see that."

I almost protested that he hadn't seen it: that I had pointed it out, but I didn't seem to be particularly important right now.

I saw Jeroniri's eyes go to Rhett, and then to narrow. I could swear I heard the prickle of his skin as Rhett the lizard started to sweat.

"That's ridiculous-"

"So why did you let an inexperienced youngster take your drugs, Rhett? It's a question I should have asked more insistently."

"I didn't think he'd get attacked," Rhett said, his voice tight. "Come on, it was just bad luck."

"All a coincidence?" Jeroniri asked, and his voice sounded quiet, and friendly, and dangerous.

"Yeah."

"I don't believe you, Rhett."

There was another silence, a longer one this time. Rhett seemed to have run out of things to say. He was blank and terrified.

Jeroniri, on the other hand, looked like he was only beginning; like he was poised to do something terrible. I felt a little ill. Was he going to have Rhett killed?

And then Axel moved slightly, and the drug-lord looked back at him, and something softened. He gave a sigh.

"I don't want anything more to do with you, or any harm or death. You wanted to persuade me to harm the one person who really mattered, and I nearly did it." He shook his head, and waved a hand towards Rhett. "Just go. I don't want to see you again. Find another city and another living, Rhett."

Rhett stared at him, blankly, until my favourite bald friend decided he'd been there long enough. He walked over and took Rhett's arm. He marched him to the door.

Jeroniri leaned back in his chair. "I want to know everything about you," he said to Axel, and at that point I felt a rush of fear. What was I doing, standing there? They needed to save Loco!

"Axel," I said, urgently. "Some of his men went to kill Luca. Your brother's in danger."

Axel looked at me, a flicker of worry crossing his face. "Why would they want to hurt Luca?"

"Revenge, nothing more," Jeroniri said, and shook his head. "I'm sorry. I didn't... I should never have agreed."

He moved towards his screen, and typed for a few moments.

"There," he said, with a smile. "I've given the order to leave off. I've summoned them home."

I had to step forward to see Axel, who was now smiling brilliantly and looking like some kind of an angel.

"I knew you weren't the person they all said," he whispered.

The magnetic draw between them had a strong hint of lust in it now. I suddenly felt like I was intruding.

"Let me show you around my empire," Jeroniri said, suddenly, standing up. He glanced at me in confusion for a second. "Miss... Taylor. You're free to go. I have no argument with you. I'm sorry for making you miss your flight."

I couldn't move for a few seconds. "That's it?" I asked, not quite believing it.

"I don't want to do business this way any more," he said, with a strange, tired smile. "I've opened my eyes at last."

But his eyes didn't look open; they looked drugged. He looked back at Axel and didn't seem able to focus on anything else.

"Are you sure they got your message?" I asked, as the big stooge moved towards me. "Are you sure Luca's safe?"

"Of course they did," Jeroniri said, with a laugh. "They're under orders to read everything that comes from me, immediately."

Yes, I thought, with a creeping fear. But will they obey you when they're out for revenge?

"Could you make sure?" I asked, as the big guy tried, gently to manoeuvre me towards the door. I craned to see around him. "It's not worth risking. Axel, he needs to make sure. It's your brother."

"Don't worry," Jeroniri said, confidently. "They'll do as they're told. They all do."

Axel gave me a brief, beaming smile.

"It's all right. He wouldn't let anyone do anything to harm me."

And in that moment, I saw what was awful in what I did. I saw the all-consuming nature of that connection, and that love. I saw the way I had been abandoned and left behind time after time. It didn't just touch them: it took them over. And nothing else had a chance of filtering through in that first rush of passion, and not a great deal later. They were gloriously happy, but Axel had lost a part of himself in that magnetic union.

My thoughts went to Luca, who might be out there already, driving into danger without knowing. And I could suddenly feel him, driving northwards at speed, a pulsing, urgent danger pushing at me from the place where he was.

Oh god. Oh, god, please let me be able to help him.

"Axel!" I called. "Axel! He's still in danger."

The big guy was pushing me towards the door as Axel said faintly, "It's all right, honestly."

I have to tell him. I have to phone him and warn him...

And then I remembered with a feeling like ice in my gut that the bald guy still had my cell-phone.

"Call him!" I shouted, as I was forced outside, not gently any more. "Call him, Axel!"

The door slammed, and with an electronic sound it locked.

I HATE WRITING about this part. I don't want to, but I know that I need to. I need to tell it to some blank pages if nothing else. I need to finish it.

I tried to stop the big guy from forcing me out of the house, but there was nothing I could do against his size. He didn't even argue with me; just picked me up across his shoulder so I couldn't draw breath to shout, and carried me down to the courtyard.

"You need to talk to your boss," I pleaded, wheezing for air, after he put me down. "You need to tell him that Luca is in danger! It'll kill Axel if anything happens to him."

"Mr. Jeroniri doesn't want to be disturbed," he said, and he pressed a button inside the door. I glanced around, and saw the gates swinging open. "You can find your own way out."

And then he closed the door in my face.

I stood there for maybe a year. Or maybe it was only a second or two. A second or two in which Luca moved closer to danger and the urgent pulsing grew stronger.

What am I going to do? Fuck. What can I do?"

It was when I turned that my eyes fell on the car we'd arrived in. It was low-slung, dark grey, and looked like an animal waiting to run. The door was standing open, the keys inserted neatly into the ignition, like it was meant for me.

This had better be fate talking, I thought as I ran towards it, and clambered in.

It had been months since I'd driven, and then only patchily. I'd never seen the point in running a car in Boston, and Fernando might have been happy to buy one, but it would have been a waste of his fortune when I cycled or walked or took the sub.

Starting up the engine and letting out the clutch felt like one of those dreams where you have to drive and you don't know how. The fear running through me only made it worse, until I almost felt like I was having an out-of-body-experience as I careened out of the gate and into the alley.

I've never driven so fast in my life. I hit ninety driving up the alley to cut back onto Comm Ave, and then I took on the stream of traffic like a madwoman.

It's not my car. It doesn't matter if I dent it or get a ticket, I said to myself, on repeat. I tried not to think about having a major crash as I undertook and overtook, and ignored every turning life at each intersection.

I could feel Luca, terrifyingly far away and moving almost as quickly. But he was alive still. I just had to drive. Somehow I would have to get there or... or I couldn't think about anything else. I had to get there.

I didn't hit any real traffic until I was north of the Charles, into Cambridge and closing the gap. There was a line of cars waiting to turn west onto Route 28. There must have been some kind of an event going on out that way, because I was stuck behind two lanes of traffic vying to push in on each other when all I wanted to do was get past them and go straight on.

I was crawling, and Luca was drawing away again, the feeling of threat stronger and stronger like a siren.

"Please," I whispered, to nothing, or to something unknown. Maybe to whatever power had given me this devastating touch of mine. "Please let him be ok. I don't even care if I lose him, as long as he lives. Please just let him live."

I could see clear road ahead of the lines of cars, but they weren't moving. Too many of them were trying to force their way onto Route 28, and we had all but stopped. I realised that the inside lane was actually moving more quickly, because it was easier to make the turn, and I shifted over.

"Fuck," I said, as I was forced to stamp on the brakes by a car cutting in two ahead. And then the last feeling of care about anything else left me. I spun the wheel and pulled the car up onto the concrete sidewalk that ran down the centre of the road. The bottom of the gleaming machine's chassis scraped over the concrete, but I put my foot down and ignored it, praying there were no cops about to stop me.

I was past the remaining cars in seconds. I didn't care that there were fifty enraged motorists blasting their horns behind me: there was open road.

I floored the accelerator. I don't think I've ever done that before, and just then it felt like flying. I hit the slip-road for the interstate at eighty and I'd passed the hundred mark by the time I joined the outside lane. I don't think if I'd been driving any less of a car that I'd have stayed on the road, but it was a beautiful machine and it did the work for me as I hit one-twenty; one-thirty; one-fifty.

It was like an arcade-game at that speed. I was seeing obstacles come up and swerving around them in seconds. In memory, it's terrifying, but all I could feel was the terror of losing Luca.

Come on. Come on.

I became aware, suddenly, that the point I was following had slowed. Luca must have turned off the interstate and into where the warehouses were.

No, I thought, willing the car to go more quickly. I was so close. If they were waiting for him...

Please. Please. Just let him live. Just let him live. Please.

I was half a mile away when I felt the danger rise to a critical point, and I cried out in pain, my foot coming off the accelerator at last.

And then another feeling replaced it, a magnetic feeling that only fear had masked from me. In my mind there was a point of light that had reached Loco.

I was hauling the protesting car off the interstate and into a slip-road when I felt the danger suddenly evaporate, and in its place the unmistakeable feeling of two points coming together.

I almost drove into them both, but I managed to brake in time. Luca was tearing at the door of a car, one that looked like it must have smashed into his beat-up old machine and pushed it into the side of the warehouse. I felt something in me snap as he leaned in, and the two points of the magnet touched.

I tried to look away, to think about something else. Anything else. I tried to work out what had happened, and realised that drawing her to him had meant her car veering off the road out of control. There was a foot protruding from under the edge of the mangled remains of Luca's car, one attached only vaguely to a leg that wore black denim, and I didn't need to have seen what happened: how Luca had climbed out of his car to meet Jeroniri's men, and how the woman driver had smashed into his car a moment later and forced it into his two waiting attackers.

I was there watching as, gently, Luca lifted the red-haired young woman out of the driver's seat and sat her on the ground a little way from the car. She was staring at him in mute adoration, and he was looking back at her in just the same way.

They didn't even see me as I turned the car around and headed back out onto the Interstate and away.

31

UNRAVELLING

So in some ways I deserve this. This feeling that's like I've had half of me ripped out. Or maybe I don't deserve any of it, but there was nothing else I could do.

I'm trying so hard to take pleasure out of the fact that he lived. I have to accept that it was what I asked for, and that something heard me. That I saved him for him, and not for me. Which I guess is what you do when you're actually in love and not just wanting to be.

It snowed last night. I can tell from the way the dawn light is rising. It has a blue-white glimmer to it that tells of snowball fights and Christmas. Or maybe just of arctic wastelands and bitter cold.

I know what I'm going to do now. Everything I thought about staying is wrong. It was founded on the stupidest hope ever: that I might actually get to keep someone.

I choose Mars, instead. I choose to leave this planet, and to be a pioneer. I choose the chance of never feeling that way about anyone ever again, and it being a blessing because I can't feel this way, either.

I'm going to call them later on. I'm going to ask whether I

can join the program now, and work with them on flight paths and bioengineering. I'm going to leave this place behind.

I know that it'll mean missing people. I'll miss my Mom and Fernando like crazy if I choose another world, but the truth is they don't need me. Not with that crazy, obsessive, perfect love that I created between them.

And I'll miss people here, too. I'll miss Maria and Fiona, despite their lack of time for me. I'll miss Eva's advice and guidance as my mentor. I'll even miss Brad, my stupid ex-boyfriend.

I'm not going to let myself think about Luca. It's too much right now.

It's light, and I need to leave my room. I need to be out in the snow, even though I don't really have anywhere to go. But maybe I won't feel so empty when I'm not here, realising that I never slept with him here; never curled up around him and let him envelope me in warmth; and that I never will.

I WENT TO CAMPUS. It wasn't a decision, really. I just walked for a while, and found myself crossing the river, trying to breathe in some of the beautiful, sun-lit and snow-whitened morning but feeling like it was nothing more than a picture. I couldn't touch it, and it couldn't touch me.

I stopped in the middle of the bridge and looked down at the flowing water. It looked gloopy, icy - deadly. It looked inviting.

But then that little sarcastic inner voice of mine piped up.

You're really living the cliché here. Are you going to wallow in self-pity for the rest of your short life, or are you going to woman the fuck up?

It was enough to make me start walking again, even though it was a half-hearted voice which didn't really sound like mine.

MIT was as empty and as pretty as a National Geographic shot. The main avenue was a gorgeous, untouched field of snow.

I hesitated before starting to walk down it, thinking how sad it was to wreck it.

I guess it'll get wrecked anyway.

I began crunching through it, taking a grim satisfaction from the sound and the sheer whiteness I was walking through.

About halfway down, my cell buzzed. I glanced at it, for some reason hoping it was Luca even though I'd blocked his number to save us both from the apologetic phone-calls.

It wasn't a number I recognised. I frowned. Was he being clever? Had he borrowed a phone in order to get through and tell me how sorry he was? How much I'd meant to him?

But I didn't think he had. I knew how it was when my exes got gripped by the touch. They only half-bothered even to contact me, and the rest of the time they were lost in adoration. I was positive he wouldn't have had time for thinking through any kind of complex plan, and that he wouldn't care enough any more.

Don't think about it. Don't think.

I answered the call with my heart pounding even so.

"Cally, it's Brandon."

"Errr... hi. How did you...?"

"Sorry for calling," he said quickly, awkwardly. "Luca messaged me your number after he told Axel to leave. He said I should get in touch with you instead of his brother if I wanted to know what was going on."

Thanks, Loco, I thought. Managing to cause me trouble after you've gone.

Unfortunately, pretending to be angry at him didn't help the pain at hearing his name, and the want to have him there with me.

"Look, I'm worried about Axel," Brandon went on, when I couldn't find anything to say. "I talked to him, and... with all the nova stuff going on, I needed him here. He said he was coming back, and then I - I haven't heard from him and he won't answer his phone. Do you know what's going on?"

I remembered, for the first time, some of my conversation with Jeroniri during that day I wanted to forget. Axel had come back for Brandon. And then I thought, *Asshole*.

"You nearly got him killed," I said. "Do you realise that? Luca sent him away for a reason. He was in danger. And because you told him you needed him, he came back and got picked up by the people who were looking for him and his brother."

"I don't know anything about anyone looking for him," he said, stiffly, immediately offended. "I just told him how I felt. It was up to him to choose."

I wanted to say more, but I realised that he was going to find out that he'd lost Axel pretty soon. It was enough punishment, even if he hadn't treated him well.

I sighed. "True, but he's impressionable. It's worth being careful with people like him."

"I will be," Brandon said, quickly. "I know that now."

I knew it wasn't up to me to tell him that his boyfriend had fallen for a drug baron and was now living happily ever after with him. So partly to change the subject, I asked, "What's happened with the supernova, then?"

"You haven't heard?" he asked, with obvious excitement. "Eta Carinae went fully nova, but extraordinarily the stars both survived. Major and minor alike. So we now have a new binary system, with one giant red dwarf which is now almost touching the smaller white dwarf. It's stable, and it's fascinating."

I couldn't tell you why, but where everything else had hurt me but let me hold it together, that broke me utterly. I was already crying as I said, "Good for them," and then hung up, unable to even say goodbye.

I didn't know where to go or what to do. There was nothing I could think of that could take away this feeling. I would fly home tomorrow on my adjusted flights, and I knew I would carry it with me.

I realised I'd been walking round and round a tree as I talked to Brandon, leaving an ever deeper trail of footprints in a trench around its base.

I need to go home, I thought, and turned back towards the gates.

My eyes were full of tears and pretty useless, but even I could see the figure who was walking rapidly down my solitary trail of footprints, leaving a second, larger set alongside them.

"Go away," I shouted at him, and turned towards the buildings again.

"Cally, wait!"

I hated hearing his voice. It was still as sexy and as open and as warm as it had been yesterday.

I didn't wait. I walked as quickly as I could, picking my feet up high in the snow.

"Cally, I've been trying to call you all night! I need to talk to you."

"Luca, please." I stopped for a moment, and turned to face him, trying to be tough Cally again. Cally-who-never-gets-upset. Cally-the-bitch. Except I couldn't be a bitch to him. "You don't need to apologise. It's what happens. I always knew it would."

"I'm not trying to apologise," he said, taking four rapid steps towards me and grabbing my arm. "I'm trying to tell you that it isn't what you think."

"I saw you," I whispered. "And I felt it happen. You fell for her and she fell for you. Like always."

"And it was like being bathed in light," he said, nodding. "Everything went fuzzy and strange and I felt soft and fascinated and protective towards her. And then you revved your engine getting back onto the interstate and I turned and saw you. I remembered you. And you know what I got to understand about everything you've been afraid of? Of all that amazing, life-changing, dramatic love that was going to hit me? It had already happened. In the sports cafe of this place, when I threw a ball into your face."

He couldn't. He couldn't love me when I'd made him love her. He couldn't help it.

He drew in close to me, his breath making warm clouds in the air between us.

"Stop looking like you're trying to see through me," he said, with a smile that made me go weak right through my body. "There's nothing to see through. I love you. I'm crazy about you, despite the fact that you're a mean and horrible person, and despite the fact that you made my brother fall in love with the head of a drugs empire."

"Really?" I asked, in a whisper that made me sound like a child. "But what about her? You still love her."

Loco shook his head. "I don't. I don't know if knowing what happened armed me somehow, but as soon as I thought of you, that was it. The spell had broken, and we both just felt a little bit awkward. I helped her get medical attention and talked to the cops for several hours, and that was it." He put a hand up to the side of my head, his fingers sliding into my hair. It was the most wonderful thing I'd ever felt. "Free choice still exists, even when you and your weird power is in the world. And I choose you."

And he kissed me.

That kiss, that soft, melting, hot, intense, dazzling kiss; that kiss right there; that was the moment that smashed the wall of ice I'd built up around myself. I felt it happen, and as terrifying as it was, I felt nothing but happiness.

I ended up crying on him for a few minutes afterwards, all wrapped up in a gorgeous hug.

"Am I forgiven for Axel?" I asked, once my voice was back.

"Ah, well, I wouldn't go that far..." he said, and then grinned down at me. "He seems to be a good influence on Mr. Jeroniri, as far as he tells me. Which is a refreshing change from all the no-good guys who've influenced him."

"Soul-mates," I said, with a smile. "There's something to be said for them."

"Ah, I think they're over-rated," he said, and kissed me again. "Now," he went on, "I don't want to ruin the moment, which, let's face it, is lovely enough to put on a Christmas card and sell, but if we don't go somewhere warm soon I think my balls might actually freeze and drop off."

I laughed at him. "OK," I said, "somewhere warm it is." And then I gave him one last kiss for good measure, savouring the heat and the taste of him. "I love you," I said. "I love you."

EPILOGUE

Luca tried to draw me to lean against him but I resisted, and settled for grabbing his hand and holding it tightly. He gave me a slow smile.

"Is Cally a little nervous?"

"Of course I am! How can you not be?"

He gave a one-shouldered shrug. "They're going to love me. Look at me. I'm every parent's dream son-in-law. I go to college, I work out, and I've totally thawed out their ice queen daughter. They're probably going to thank me for saving you from a lonely old age surrounded by cats and talking crazy. Hey, ow!"

I didn't stop prodding him hard in the side until he let go of my other hand and, laughing, trapped both of my arms between his hands.

"You did not thaw me out," I said, trying not to smile. "I'm still an ice queen. And I'll freeze your ass if you don't behave."

"Hmm," he said, considering. "Does that involve any more of what we did last night?"

I felt my face growing warm, a mixture of embarrassment that the cab driver could hear him and the very hot memory of a long night with little sleep. For a moment I was back in my bed, with Luca over me and inside me, his mouth and mine pressed together. It was so vivid that I could feel my abdomen and groin all tightening in anticipation.

"No, it does not," I said, but I grabbed another one of those kisses from him. The hot, soft, wet kind that is one of the sexiest things alive.

"OK," he said, afterwards, with a slight sigh. "I'll stop teasing you, because if I arrive at your parents' house with a hard-on, I don't think the Loco charm will work."

I gave him a triumphant smile, and then tried to think about things other than nerves or last night.

"Were you nervous yesterday?" I asked, after a moment of silence. "Before you took me to see your mom?"

"Not really," he said, considering. "I was worried you'd find it hard. Not because you wouldn't want to be there but... I know I get a little emotional sometimes at how different it is there from an ideal Christmas. You know?"

I did know. It had made me sad, even though I'd been totally happy at being trusted enough to be let into that final part of his life.

Luca had prepared me for the trip, but it had shaken me, driving West toward Albany and then diverging to a small, roadside town that probably only existed because of the hospital. The snow there had been piles of black-stained sludge on the sidewalk, and even the scenery was flat and depressing for a few square miles.

The hospital was gated, and I guessed that its occupants would be sitting out in the garden come summer. In winter, it was a bare, lifeless forecourt with a few spindly trees not doing enough to hide the utilitarian, 1970s hospital building behind.

Inside, it had smelled of bleach and old carpets. The nurse who showed us up to Mrs. Veste's room was at least a little cheering. His chubby face smiled easily, and he exchanged jokes with a few residents on the way past.

I'd got to the doorway with Luca, and suddenly been scared to go in. I'd been afraid of the reality of Luca's Mom, who had been beaten into a drug-dependency, and gradually descended into psychosis. I was afraid of how this must hurt him.

But when he drew me inside, gently, I felt nothing but a rush of sympathy for the frail, once-blonde woman who was gazing at a small hanging Christmas star that was twisting left and right in front of the window, sending fractured gold light across the walls.

"Mom," Luca had said gently, and gone to kiss her. He had waited while she slowly dragged her eyes away from the star, and then focused on him. "I want you to meet someone."

We'd had our own Christmas there, together. And it had been hard, and heart-breaking, but it had also at times been wonderful, like the moment when Luca's Mom had finally picked the loose wrapping off the earrings her son had bought her, and smiled at them in delight.

So I knew what he meant. It hadn't been ideal; but it had been important.

I nodded, and leaned in to kiss his neck. "I know."

"I didn't worry what she'd think of you," he said. "I knew she'd love you. She always had a talent for seeing through defences. For seeing the good in people."

"Hey, I wasn't defensive," I said, lightly.

"No," he agreed, with a warm grin. "You weren't. You were perfect."

"Well I'm sure you'll be perfect too," I said.

"Good. So you can stop death-gripping my hand any time you like."

. . .

I FELT ALMOST ashamed of the size and beauty of the house Fernando had bought my Mom. They'd strung up some tiny white lights across the trees on the drive, and there was a huge, all-natural wreath on the front door. There was no snow here, but there was growing twilight, and a crescent moon hanging over the house, and a single star visible in the dark blue sky. It looked idyllic. Like the Christmas Eve you always want as a kid but never seem to quite get.

The cab-driver helped us out with our cases, and then was gone into the night, leaving it strangely quiet. I guessed my Mom and Fernando were in the big kitchen at the back and hadn't heard us arrive.

OK. You're going to introduce him to them, I thought. It's a really good thing.

And yet, somehow, the familiar panic seized me and I couldn't bring myself to rap on the door.

"What's the matter?" Luca asked, looping his arms loosely around me. He peered at my face. "Are you having a relapse?"

"No, no," I said, even though he was almost right. "I'm just... it's such a big thing. I've never got to this part of things. It always... I just... I know you love me. But what if you fall in love with someone else? What if you meet someone you love more? I know you didn't want the red-head but there are other people."

"And what if you do?" he countered, gently. "I've thought about that, too. But I think it's worth the risk."

"But it's not the same," I argued.

"Yes, it is," he said, firmly, but with a grin. "It's exactly the same. That's the wonderful thing about it. You're taking just the same risk I am, and you're doing it because that's what people do when they're in love. Because being afraid of losing it is one of the things that makes it mean something."

For a long time I looked back at him, the panic gradually easing at his steady, still-dangerous gaze.

"I hate it when you're right," I said, and prodded him in the stomach again.

"I know."

I wanted to kiss him, for everything. For making the fear go away; for still being here now, when I thought I'd lost him; for just being him.

But as I leaned up towards him, there was the strangest feeling in the air. It was like something profound had changed a long way away, and we'd felt the shockwaves here.

I was immediately breathless, and my heart was hammering in my chest.

"Did you feel that?" I asked.

I could see from his eyes that he had. They were scanning the horizon, looking for something.

"Yeah," he said, slowly. "It's... it felt like how it does when you do your thing, or I do mine. Only different from either."

And for the first time I thought of the possibility that there were other people like us; other people who did strange things to the people around them, and affected the world in unnatural ways.

"There's someone like us out there," I said, feeling strangely jealous. Instinctively I disliked the idea of there being anyone else, of it not just being us.

"There is," he agreed, and then he focused on me again, and he smiled. "But that's a problem for another day. Right now, we have a turkey and what I'm hoping is a shit-ton of potatoes to vanquish."

"You'd better believe it," I said, and despite the nagging worry, I knew he was right all over again. Right now, this was all that mattered. I grabbed his hand, took a breath, and knocked loudly on the door.

Printed in Great Britain
by Amazon